Fus

Fusco, John
Dog Beach

Also by John Fusco

Paradise Salvage

DOG BEACH

John Fusco

A Touchstone Book
Published by Simon & Schuster
New York   London   Toronto   Sydney   New Delhi

Touchstone
A Division of Simon & Schuster, Inc.
1230 Avenue of the Americas
New York, NY 10020

First Touchstone hardcover edition September 2014

TOUCHSTONE and colophon are registered trademarks of Simon & Schuster, Inc.

For information about special discounts for bulk purchases, please contact Simon & Schuster Special Sales at 1-866-506-1949 or business@simonandschuster.com.

The Simon & Schuster Speakers Bureau can bring authors to your live event. For more information or to book an event contact the Simon & Schuster Speakers Bureau at 1-866-248-3049 or visit our website at www.simonspeakers.com. # FIC 9-9-14

Interior design by Robert Ettlin
Jacket design by Ervin Serrano
Jacket photograph © Jim Corwin/The Image Bank/Getty Images

Manufactured in the United States of America

pages cm
1. Screenwriters—Fiction. 2. Stunt performers—Fiction. 3. Mafia—Fiction.
I. Title.
PS3606.U83D64 2014
813'.6—dc23   2013049875
ISBN 978-1-4767-5034-7
ISBN 978-1-4767-5036-1 (ebook)

For JC

DOG
BEACH

PROLOGUE

He is running, eight stories up on a rusted crossbeam, when he feels it, that thing entering his bloodstream, the rush he secretly calls the Creature. The timer on the explosives—280 pounds of M112 demolition charges—is beeping down the count. Six seconds . . . his heart drums full throttle, blood rushing. His pupils dilate and everything out in front of him becomes otherworldly clear. Four seconds. He's done this for half a lifetime. For what? Money? For the thrill of making some A-lister look good on-screen? Or for the raw adrenaline dump, that addiction to the Creature in his bloodstream? It always surges harder when he's unwired, like now. Two seconds . . . but he's too far from the end of the beam and the timer tells him he's not going to make it; that's when he comes alive, racing out ahead of the shock front, pulsing with that confidence that's carried him through his private war against gravity, the car crashes, the full-burns, and the impossible high-falls. Like the one from the bridge in Macau that damaged his L4 vertebrae in '86. No matter how bad life has turned out, how many bones he's broken, how many ex-wives want what's left of the pieces, he is still Louie Mo: a *legend among Hong Kong stuntmen. Even if it isn't the '80s anymore.*

As the building erupts—his eardrums rupture and ring—he feels himself launch from his body. No nets, no wires. This one's on him. And there's that question, somewhere just under the wild hum of the Creature and the ringing in his ears: Did I die this time?

1

PALM SPRINGS, MAGIC HOUR

Louie Mo sat in the passenger seat, peering through tinted aviators at the big hotel. The car, a beat-up Chevy Impala, smelled of cigarettes, aftershave, and a Supreme Croissant.

"Shit, this mother's hot," Dutch said, clawing the Styrofoam cup. "If I spilled it on me, I could sue Jack in the Box for ten mill."

Louie glanced at her, the girl he usually just called Driver, but his mind was still fixed on the Marriott. "Too many people sue," he said in his broken English.

"What?"

"Too many people, they sue."

"Yeah, well, just think about it," she said. "We could buy a house and you could get your hip replacement. Wouldn't have to take generic painkillers, could get the real ones."

"Not right."

"Not right." She laughed, smoke escaping out a pierced nostril. She edged the coffee to her pout but didn't sip.

"You're about to go in there and break somebody's legs and you have moral issues with suing Jack in the Box?"

"The people inside are no good people," Louie reasoned. He checked his cell phone, a constant tic.

"And the people who hired you, are they good people?"

"Be quiet now." He slipped his phone inside his white denim jacket. "What room again?"

"Four-twelve."

Louie opened the glove box, removed a pair of metal nunchaku. He never took a gun, and even the nunchaku were simply for backup. "Okay, here I go."

"Time is money."

"Lock up."

"I'll be right here, yo. Call my cell if you take another way out."

Louie sighed, popped his collar up like Elvis. Dutch thought about that now: With those outsized amber glasses and white jacket, Louie Mo kind of resembled an aging Chinese Elvis. He even walked like one, despite a slight limp, as he moved past lit-up palm trees and the big hotel marquee:

WELCOME—SPORTS MEMORABILIA
CONVENTION
June 4–6

Dutch watched him go, with only slight disdain for the way things were. Actually, she was kind of used to it now. She sipped the coffee, considered it still hot enough to burn her leg and justify calling 911, but "Not right," says Louie Mo. If Elvis was the King of Rock 'n' Roll what would Louie Mo be? she wondered. An old '80s song came into her head: "The King of Pain."

Perfect.

• • •

On the fourth floor of the Marriott, Louie spotted a room service tray—half-eaten spaghetti carbonara, two empty wine-glasses—left outside some guest's door. He picked it up in careful silence and moved down to Room 412. He buzzed the door and called out, "Room service," in his broken English.

The guy who cracked the door was slight and un-healthy-looking with sideburns that could house mole rats. Behind him, a fat man overwhelmed a chair while a third guy, blond and fine-boned, arranged sports memorabilia on one of the queen-size beds.

"We didn't order no room service," said Sideburns, turning to look at the fat man straining the chair. "You order—"

Louie slammed the tray into his face, kicked him in the solar plexus. The fat man, never leaving his chair, clawed for something inside his windbreaker. A gun, small and Austrian-made. Louie's spinning heel kick got there first, crushing the guy's mandible. Completing a full spin, Louie intercepted the third man, trapped his elbow. Broke it. Then he did the same to a knee with a low, practical sidekick. Nothing fancy.

A toilet flushed and a fourth man entered, towel in

5

hands. He stood blinking for a second then dropped the towel and grabbed awkwardly for a baseball bat among the sports prizes. Louie spun with a back fist, whipping his first two knuckles into the man's temple. The Batter crumpled into the narrow space between the queen bed and the wall: 2.3 seconds. That's all it took, the entire fight.

"Fuck," Louie said, his second-favorite English word.

He turned to the arranged items on the beds, whispering strange American sports names to himself as he tried to remember what he came to retrieve. He tossed a framed team photo aside, then a scrapbook full of baseball cards, a hockey stick, a catcher's mask, a shadowbox containing a trophy ring, and, propped up on the bank of pillows: an Oakland Raiders jersey, number 99, signed in Sharpie and framed. Grabbing the collectible, Louie hurried to the second bed just as the Batter lifted his head, groggy. Louie punched him in the face then took inventory. Almost immediately, he spotted it: A football resting on a mahogany stand. He checked the signature, claimed it.

Stepping over the guy whose face and shirt were splattered in carbonara, Louie tried to calm his breathing and get out with the items. He darted into the hallway, looked back. The third man was up on his knees now, trying to operate his iPhone with his unbroken left hand.

• • •

"What about the helmet?" Dutch said, throwing the Chevy into a U-turn.

"No helmet."

Louie was looking over his shoulder at the Marriott, where something was going down; men were scrambling, a security guard was running, first one way, then the other. When Louie turned back around, he saw a black Escalade lurching out from the parked cars and trying to block their path.

Dutch slammed the brakes, dropped into a reverse 180, nearly hitting the lit-up marquee. Another security guard, a powerfully built black woman, stormed the passenger side, yelling. Louie opened his door, used it like a gladiator's shield, hit her square. He winced when he saw her roll. He didn't realize it was a woman, but there was no time now for sentiment.

Dutch made a crisp quarter turn, pulled the E-brake, and skid. Her bare right foot—ankle bracelet and chipped nail polish—flattened the accelerator. She shuffle-steered between two U-Hauls, jumped the curb, and gunned it west. Out on Frank Sinatra Drive, she lifted her eyes to the rear-view. No police lights. Good. She touched a lighter to a cigarette, maintained a steady pace.

Louie, breathing normally now, turned back to the street and opened the glove box. Rummaging through clutter, he found a vial, empty. He dug through several other spent pre-scriptions, finally coming up with a little bottle that rattled with promise.

"Those are mine," Dutch said, and when Louie stared at her, she explained, "For my female problem."

"I have female problem too," Louie said. "All my life. Didn't know they had pills for it."

"Very funny. You should get off on Jack Benny Road, do comedy."

Louie shoved the vial back in, slammed the glove box shut. Everything was hurting him, from his injured lumbar to the Achilles' tendon he once tore jumping between sub-way cars, a long time ago, on *Fist of Vengeance*. But it was mostly his hip flexors from sitting in the Chevy for too damn long.

Dutch looked at him now, her hazel eyes glazed from the afterburn of epinephrine. It was the thing they had in common: adrenaline junkies, both.

"Fucking Louie Mo." She laughed. "Some enforcer."

"Man has gun, almost I get killed."

"Dude, you're like the Tin Man."

"What is Tin Man?"

"*Wizard of Oz*. The Tin Man was all broken parts of rusted metal, rattled when he walked."

Louie Mo squinted at her over the rims of his aviators like she was speaking in obscure haiku. His surly, bee-stung eyes, offset by a boyish glint, forever amused her.

"He went all the way to Oz," she explained, "trying to find a heart, but then he realized that he had one all along."

"I don't want a heart," Louie said. "I want a Vicodin."

Dutch laughed, Palm Springs now in her rearview mirror.

2

DOG BEACH, MALIBU

"Clusterfuck," Troy said, sitting in front of his twenty-inch monitor and watching a year's worth of bad acting and incoherent narrative. Not even Final Cut Pro could make sense of it.

"A Film by Troy Raskin," he said, with all the dark ceremony of signing a suicide note. "Produced by Avi Ghazaryan — which means Lucifer spelled backward in Armenian."

"Careful, bro," said Durbin. "Ghazaryan can walk through this door any minute."

"It's got narrative problems," T-Rich said. "But I wouldn't go so far as to call it a disaster."

"*I* would," said Malone. "I think it actually reinvents the disaster film. Turns it on its fucking ear."

The Malibu locals called Las Flores "Dog Beach," so Troy and his housemates named their two-story beach crib the Dog House, called themselves the Dogs of Entropy. Durbin, the weasel-thin, aspiring screenwriter, tended to

JOHN FUSCO

hold down his own corner of the house, an iPad and a bean bag chair his only tools. T-Rich, African American with red-framed glasses, was an NYU buddy of Troy's and the new-media artist in the posse; his bachelor's thesis was shot entirely on a smartphone.

Then there was Malone. Redheaded, ginger scruff on his chin, baggy plaid shorts always halfway down his crack. He referred to himself as a UCLA dropout. In reality, he'd been kicked off campus for turning a trash barrel on the quad into a volcano for a thirty-second experimental film he called *Fra Diavolo*. These days the pyro busied himself crewing for Troy, handling all the torrents of fake blood and bullets and Fuller's Earth on Avi Ghazaryan's *Slash*.

Their Dog Beach neighbors—the actor Gary Busey on one side, a reality show producer on the other—called them the rich film school brats, even though all four had been out of film school for at least two years, and none was really rich; most of them had student loans weighing on them like brick vests.

Nor did they own the beach house. The producer Avi Ghazaryan was leasing it to Troy in exchange for a promised film. The project, said to be based on an original idea of Ghazaryan's, was called *Slash*.

"We're not tenants here," Troy said now, his spirits sinking deeper. "We're hostages."

"As long as Avi sees his daughter getting screen time, he's happy, bro," Durbin said. "All good."

Troy stared futilely at Zoe Ghazaryan on the monitor. "She'd make a wooden Indian seem compelling."

10

Dark and striking, Zoe wasn't exactly hard for the Dogs to look at. Not for the first six months, at least. Now her footage was driving them bug-shit; her voice was a constant nasal drone from Troy's speakers, her outsized butt a self-conscious intrusion in the beach house; the monitor could barely contain it.

She had potential, T-Rich observed the first time he watched her escape from a zombie, running and bouncing like Meghan Fox. "But she seems kind of torn. I mean, between her love for herself and her love for the camera."

"Maybe we should put her in the Malone Zone," Durbin said. This was code talk at the Dog House, a kind of arcane lingo. In the lexicon of the Dogs, the Malone Zone meant to blow something to smithereens by way of Malone's homemade squibs or converted M-80s, all of which he usually lit with the glowing end of a joint. As they chanted it now, in unison, Malone squinted and grinned, proud to be the object of tribal incantation.

11

Troy froze on Zoe's pretty face and left her there, but the posing was too much. He blackened the screen, stared into the void, numb. "I can't do this fucking movie."

"You have to," Durbin said over his shoulder. "Or you'll owe him thirteen months' rent, and what is it—a hundred and eighty grand for his investment?"

"I wouldn't want to be six figures in debt to that dude," T-Rich said. "Who knows who his investors are?"

Troy turned from the dead monitor and looked at him. It was how his former classmate said it, almost chilling.

"What do you mean?"

"*Dude*," Malone said, "have you seen some of the daughter's boyfriends she brings to the set? They look like the cast of *Sons of Anarchy*."

Troy ruminated on this for a moment then swiveled from his seat. He grabbed a bag of stale bread and prepared to feed the seagulls. It was something he did lately when he got anxious.

"Look," he said, throwing open the French doors. "There's nothing sexier than a Go movie. But a few days in, you feel like you've had the sex. It was great, but now you just want to go home."

"We wouldn't know about Go movies," Durbin said. "You're the only one who's getting made."

"And getting laid," said T-Rich.

"Yeah. Seriously. What is up with that?" said Malone.

"I never should've signed on to this fucking movie. Should've just taken out a loan and garage-banded that old-school action thing."

T-Rich watched with a kind of fascination as Troy flung bread crusts to the four directions. "*The Rage?*"

"*The Cage.*"

"You ever finish that script?"

"Ninety pages. Just need a third-act banger."

"Wait. Is that the John Woo meets early fifties Western noir meets *Run, Lola, Run*?"

"Jesus, Durbin, you just gave me a boner. That could be the poster."

"Well, maybe after you finish *Slash*—"

"FUCK *SLASH*!" Troy erupted over the surf. A guy jogging by wheeled like he'd been stung by a kelp fly. Troy did a double take, watched the guy trip down the shore. The Dogs stood, waiting for Troy to identify the jogger as some character actor with a video store legacy; he was forever spotting movie people from the porch, even obscure ones, like the director of a Dutch art film, or the French actress who hadn't done a thing since the late '70s. Durbin once said that Troy had a mind like IMDb. T-Rich believed it was more like an idiot-savant tic, like Rain Man playing poker. But Troy made no such identification of the annoyed jogger now. He just stood in the open French doors, looking gaunt and defeated as seagulls descended all around him. The bread was gone, the plastic bag wilted.

"Who are you yelling at?" the voice was deep and even, a man's voice piercing the chatter of mere boys. Avi Ghazaryan, tall and slim in a tracksuit, adjusted his dark eyes to the beach house light.

"Avi," Troy said, edging inside and closing the doors to keep out the gull noise.

Avi stood there, BMW keys in his hand, surveying the scene like a father checking in on the bedroom of lazy teenage sons. Behind him, a door closed. Heels clicked. Zoe entered like she owned the place. Tiny top, skinny jeans, outsized sunglasses. Her straight hair, black as a raven's wing, caught the sunlight as she went to a closet. With all the nose-up entitlement of a princess in Daddy's castle, she retrieved a yoga mat.

"Where's my movie?" Avi said, glancing at Troy's dead monitor and the mad cascade of storyboards, index cards, and dead cups from the Coffee Bean.

"What?"

Avi laughed smoothly. "*What.* I ask where is my movie, you always say the same thing: *What.* Fuck you, Troy."

"The second act needs some liposuction, that's all."

"Why don't you show me? I cut an hour of shoe leather out of *Low Tide* when Vanderbosh didn't know what to do with it. He thanked me. All the way to fucking Sundance he thanked me."

"I'd really rather not show anything yet—"

"It's been a fucking year!"

The yell startled Troy. Startled everyone.

"I—I know," Troy stammered, "but I'm experimenting with a few things that are still Jell-O and I want to nail it down first."

"Omigod, Troy," said Zoe. There it was, that Valley Girl whine. "People usually say 'nail down Jell-O' to mean something's, like, impossible. Talk about mixing your metaphors. You're such a tool."

Avi looked at Durbin, caught the struggling writer wincing up at him. When Durbin lowered his eyes back to his iPad, Avi suggested that the boys (freeloaders, he called them) go for a walk on the beach.

"I need to talk business with my director."

The guys, all but Troy, shuffled out onto the back porch, Indian-filed down the steps to the sand. Zoe stood off in the kitchen, hand on a big hip, sipping a glass of cool filtered water from the fridge.

"You have four weeks to turn in a cut," Avi said.

"What?"

"You've put me in a very bad position with my investors. Four weeks, or your schoolboy ass is out of my house. And you pay me back every fucking penny, I don't care if you have to call your mother in Connecticut . . . Baby Boy Troy."

Troy did a chilled take at the name, but then Avi was gone. Zoe finished her water, left the empty glass for the tenants to clean and put away. On her way out, she went to Troy's desk, sorted through the color-coded strip board. "We shooting Monday or not?"

"Not if it rains."

"We're in Southern California, duh."

"I think we got most of your stuff, Zoe. I know we want to do reshoots on the crying scene, but we have the rest of June."

"Easy on the liposuction. If you cut anything, cut that little porn star you're fucking. The redhead from Charlie's house. She can't act her way out of a paper bag."

Zoe left the house. Troy stood there, waiting to hear the door latch. "Yeah, okay, Hepburn, you Armenian skank."

Someone touched his shoulder and he started.

"Dude," Durbin said. "What'd he say?"

The young filmmakers were back inside, forming a loose huddle. "I think he threatened me," Troy said.

"I told you," T-Rich said. "The guy is sketchy."

"You notice how he's got a vampire accent?" Malone said. "I mean like a high-end vampire. The vampire one percent."

"He's giving me four weeks."

"Or what?"

"I don't know. But I think he's tapped the phone. He knows what Alexis calls me, I mean her little nickname for me."

"Dog House is *tapped*?" Malone said.

"What's Alexis call you?" Durbin wanted to know. "Is it nasty?"

"This sucks, man." Troy clutched for more stale bread, then threw the empty bag.

Malone stood at the closet, checking on his surfboard. "What did the fourth Kardashian take out of our closet?"

"A yoga mat," said Durbin. "Troy, what are you going to do?"

"I'm going nonlinear with the structure. I'm going to baffle myself into an inspired work of lunacy. And then I'm going to run."

"Nonlinear is six years ago," T-Rich said, picking up Zoe's water glass and examining the perfect lipstick on the rim.

"Well, you have any ideas for saving this piece of shit?" Troy looked at each of them. A dog barked at the waves outside; a woman called out to someone down the beach. The seagulls returned to the porch, determined. But not a single desperate idea from the Dogs of Entropy.

Then Malone had a brainstorm: "I'd just run, bro."

3

MARINA DEL REY

The sun had been up for twenty minutes, but Louie Mo and
Dutch "the Clutch" Dupree were just waking in the front
seat. They'd spent most of the night in the dark little bar
of the Marina del Rey Hotel, drinking house cabernet and
recounting the Palm Springs gag. Both had been out of the
stunt business for years, but they still called their jobs "gags."
On her third glass, Dutch had proposed a plan for balancing
the books: deliver the signed jersey to the client but keep
the collectible football; store it in the trunk, like a treasury
bond. At first, Louie had resisted, equating this to spilling
hot coffee on your thigh and suing Jack in the Box. But
by his last glass of sour cab, he had warmed to the idea of
double-dipping. In fact, he told Dutch that she was clever.

Yet, it bothered him now as he lugged the framed Raiders jersey down onto the mooring along a crowded row of
aging yachts and sailboats. He could hear Dutch ringing a
cell phone somewhere on one of the crafts — the ringtone

was some kind of rock guitar riff—and a moment later, the client appeared. He was a hungover hulk of a man, waving Louie on board the small yacht.

Down inside the mahogany galley, Louie got a better look at Jason Banazak. At six foot six and three hundred pounds, the onetime football star was closer in size to a Kodiak bear than a human being. Dutch told him that the guy had earned a half-dozen sports awards and just as many steroid charges, firearm possessions, and date-rape scandals. Louie noted that he also had the pronounced brow ridge of a Neanderthal. Like Louie himself, Banazak's best days were far behind him and he had stopped cutting his graying curls. But it was his eyes—flat and cold—that stopped Louie short.

It wasn't that Louie was intimidated by the guy's size; he loved fighting oversized men, playthings if you've been trained in kung fu. What scared him was that wounded glaze in the ex-jock's eyes that made him feel like he was looking into a mirror.

"Where's the Super Bowl ball?"

"Couldn't find."

"What do you mean, 'Couldn't find'?"

"Could not find."

"I know every single fucking item they had in that room, and the Super Bowl ball was on a stand with a little plaque."

"Couldn't find Super Ball."

"Couldn't find Super Ball," Banazak mocked Louie's broken English, then grunted, sitting on the edge of the un-made cot near a tiny white lapdog. Louie looked around the galley, intrigued. "You live here? On boat?"

Banazak surrendered a tired nod, already counting off a fold of cash. "Did you fuck them up good, Chinaman?"

"Yes. Fuck them up very good."

Banazak glanced up, grinned with a broken front tooth. He seemed amused by this loan-out enforcer, the little Asian guy with a reputation for clearing a room. When he handed Louie the cash, Louie quickly, almost magician-like, handed back a one-hundred-dollar bill.

"Oxycodone," Louie said, surrendering a sheepish grin. "I see it. On the desk. Right over there."

It took Banazak a few foggy seconds to make the connection. Then he reached back and snagged a full vial of prescription painkillers, tossed it hard at Louie. When he caught it, Louie went dark. *Crude American asshole.* A man bluffs his way into a hotel room and beats the living crap out of four scumbags for the price of three, retrieves stolen property and delivers it to your Marina del Rey houseboat and you toss a vial of painkillers at him like he's a beggar.

Fuck you.

That's what Louie wanted to say. *You give to me, you give to me with two hands and with respect. A little humility.* But then the lapdog lifted its pink nose and began to yap. Louie drew back a step, but the apso kept barking sharply at him. Funny, Louie thought, how dogs can sense what a person's thinking. That observation cooled him down. Temper was a weakness anyway, a sign of a lesser man. He remembered the old Sifu at the Peking Opera School telling him such things when he was a child, hanging upside down from his ankles while the Sifu beat him with a rattan cane. Westerners

19

never understood Louie when he talked about Peking Opera School; they thought he'd been trained to sing and dance. The school, however, was really a boarding facility where young students—so many of them orphans or runaways—trained rigorously in acrobatics, martial arts, and tumbling skills. Louie was disciplined if nothing else. But more than anything, right now, he was just happy to have his hands on a fully loaded cylinder of relief. He also felt bad for the big, broken shell of a giant who used to wear number 99. When Louie climbed back to the sunny deck and the smell of hash browns and starter fluid, Banazak remained down in the galley, still staring at the floor.

"So sad," Louie said back in the car, going on and on about it. "So sad, this man."

"He's a rapist," Dutch said, popping an oxy. "Served time for beating up a sixteen-year-old black chick. He's forfeited any right to fair play. Fuck him."

Onward they went, like Bonnie and Clyde.

4

THE IVY

"The economics of the industry have changed," Avi Ghazaryan said in that silky, Armenian timbre. "The town used to
be paved with dumb money. You have a good idea, you get
a deal. Now? They will only make movies that come with
an underlying brand." He was sitting at a lunch table with
three Latino men and a private detective named Papagallo,
onetime "private eye to the stars."

"My daughter used to play that game Scrabble. Go to
Paramount and pitch Scrabble as a movie and you'll get a
deal. Or fucking Slinky. Go to Warners with Slinky and a
writer and you've got one on the books. One problem: You
have to pay the rights holder. So, I ask myself: How do you
pitch a brand without having to pay the rights? You ready?
Look outside the window. Do you see the little man on the
crosswalk light? Yes, you see him. The little stick-figure man.
He's also on all the pedestrian crossing signs, from here to
New York. So imagine this: An old woman is out walking

her dog in the rain. Lightning strikes the caution sign as she passes. The dog barks, they run inside. Next morning, the old woman—Kathy Bates, say—walks by the caution sign. But something's strange. The little man is gone from the sign. He's out there somewhere. And he kills. Serial killer. These guys, the town—I don't know what town, some fucking town—they bring in a bounty hunter. I can get Randy Couture. He has to hunt down the little crosswalk man, the caution sign man. It's a brand that everyone knows, but no one owns the rights to."

Avi drew a soft breath, ate a little salmon and balsamic greens, genuinely inspired. "I call this idea *Caution*. That's it. Just *Caution*. It's a pre-branded fucking hit with a nice one-word title."

"What's going on with the zombie movie?" said one of the Latinos, a handsome guy in a blazer named Hektor. Papagallo was busy with his iPhone, and this frustrated Avi; he'd expected a bigger reaction to his crosswalk-man idea, but he knew he was dealing with idiots.

"This little fuck, Troy," Avi said. "He's having an artistic tantrum. Needs more time."

"Needs more time?" said Hektor, looking at his partners. "We put in real coin, Avi. You guaranteed a return."

"One thousand percent," said an older Latino, staring warily at the talapia lunch special.

"That's right," Avi said. "As soon as this little fucker finishes the movie."

"Well, *make* him finish the movie."

"Why are we babying this guy?" the older one said. "Have Hektor go over there and show him his tattoos."

Hektor smiled at the thought. Indeed, the side of his neck facing the wall was scrimmed with elaborate ink swirls and symbols; there was little doubt that those tattoos must have covered his torso and back.

"He's just a kid," Avi said, a little embarrassed by how protective he sounded. "These kids are geniuses, but they're babies. Immature."

"Well, put him in fucking time-out," Papagallo said, looking up from his iPhone for the first time. "I know a fixer who sends out a guy. Foreign guy. Knee-breaker. Puts the fear of God in guys who don't want to write a check."

"How much?"

"Let me call my guy, but I think it's under two grand for him to put the first elbow on. Usually don't need a second."

Avi was gazing out at the little blinking crosswalk man, thinking about how he'd look in motion-capture. And then he had one of those brainstorms like the one that engendered the idea for *Slash*. In the final scene, Randy Couture should trap the Caution Man at the curb, pull his gun, and speak a line that audiences would be recalling for years: *Don't walk, motherfucker.*

"It's time," said the older Latino, still not touching the talapia. "Get a fire under this guy's ass or give us back our money. My boss wanted to invest in some Internet stuff, but Hektor loves your movies."

"The action ones, I like," Hektor said. "*Low Tide*, I like. I don't like the ones when the people talk."

"Let me tell you a little story," Avi said. "By the time Johnny Depp's next movie comes out, he's five years older but everyone wants to cast him at the same age as the last movie. That's the one thing people never understand. Making a movie is like planting an apple tree. Time and patience."

"I'd rather just buy the fucking apples at Farmer's Market," the older guy said, and Papagallo laughed.

Avi looked away from the crosswalk man, stared at Papagallo and his itchy iPhone thumb. "Okay. Call your guy. Put a little pressure on my director. But don't hurt him. Just scare him and let him know he's not in film school anymore."

Avi was up, saying good-bye, but not shaking hands. He had his Beamer's keys out, eager to call the boys at WME and get on the Paramount lot, ambush Tyler at the commissary. "Tell Tyler I want to hand him a fucking pot of gold" is what he always instructed his agents when he knew he had a eureka idea. *Caution.* It had the ring of *Taken*, and *Taken* had made two hundred million on a twenty-mill budget.

Don't walk, motherfucker. It could be the new *Go ahead, make my day.*

5

THROUGH THE OVERPASS

Driving Highway 10, Dutch had a headache, a dry mouth, and a strange yearning for pork carnitas, slow cooked like they used to do in Santa Fe. A heavy mantle of smog and haze left a residue on her windshield and that's what she blamed her headache on: L.A. Not the wine; the wine was her friend and ally. Los Angeles was the disease and this ugly stretch of freeway was the darkest part of it. No matter how many times she drove this route, she always forgot that it would soon duck beneath an overpass just north of Santa Monica and mercifully spit her out into a cleansing wash of blue sky and surfers. She always felt a false jolt of freedom, like the drab underpass was the wardrobe and Malibu was the Narnian multiverse waiting on the other side. When she glanced at Louie to see if he was feeling it too, she found him sleeping, mouth agape.

They were almost at their destination, but she let Louie sleep through a U-turn at Moonshadows Restaurant. She parked where she could find a crack between cars a few houses down from the Las Flores Beach address.

Feeling the stop, Louie came awake, said the same thing he always did: "I snore?"

"The brown house up there."

She spilled a key from an envelope, handed it over. "They said let yourself in through the gate, follow the path down to the beach, and go in through the back porch."

Louie turned the key over in his hands, assessed the duplex. It was one of the more ramshackle beach places wedged between the nicer homes, but Malibu was Malibu and ramshackle was still ten million in real estate; who knew who might live there?

"I scare this guy, right?"

"Yeah, scare his ass. Don't break it."

She looked at the address on the Jack in the Box napkin. "His name's Troy."

Louie committed the name to cloudy memory, opened his door. Dutch watched him shuffle along the side of the roaring highway. He often walked with what stunt guys called a "lifetime achievement limp," but he looked particularly sore and tired today. Still, he had that incongruous youthful stride, buoyed by white sneakers. From behind he could appear almost young, his glutes permanently hardened from five decades of martial arts. Reclining her seat back a notch, she tapped a smoke. Beautiful day. Not a bad place to sit. Maybe she'd see Tom Petty.

• • •

"Spank my ass like you're mad at it," Alexis Cain breathed, in between shrill, rhythmic calls like dolphin song.

The redhead who played a zombie in Troy's movie was sitting on him in reverse cowgirl, wearing nothing but pink Uggs because her feet were always cold. She rode him hard, slapping his leg and digging in her nails. "Spike it like a volleyball," she wailed.

From his bedroom window, Troy could see the morning haze burning off Dog Beach. Malone was out surfing, and T-Rich and Durbin wouldn't be back from Ralph's with groceries for a good hour. Dog House was all his this morning, his and the ginger's, cat-backing now like a Montana bull rider. He felt himself lurch, close to eruption. Alexis Cain knew sex like Troy knew the collected works of Abel Ferrara; the girl lived up at the Point in a large glass-and-adobe triplex owned by Charlie Sheen. She was, if the rumors at Googie's were correct, one of Charlie's girls. Not one of his porn star goddesses, but part of the farm team. She wanted to go legit, she said, but Charlie wouldn't take her seriously. This kid Troy seemed to be her best chance. If *Slash* got distribution, she could be on her way; she was young enough to start over. Young enough to play high school girls if she had to.

Troy grimaced and did the thing he'd been doing lately for staying power: He thought about scenes from his doomed movie. Almost instantly, it triggered reverse ejaculation. Sometimes even shrinkage. Thinking of profoundly vile things like the compost bucket or Zoe Ghazaryan's dialogue always helped him prolong in such moments. So he was baffled that the image of Zoe, the bane of his grueling imprisonment in the Dog House, had the opposite effect.

He spasmed.

Alexis cheered him on, her voice like helium. She must've had a volleyball fetish because she kept using terms like "spike it" and "jungle ball." Troy begged her to dismount. She was bruising his pelvis now, riding him into the springs. Finally, she pitched forward and rolled, looked up at him crazy-eyed.

"Did you film us?" she said. "Don't lie to me, Troy."

"Film us? Just now? God, no."

Troy caught a mope of disappointment on her face, but before he could analyze it, he heard the sound; they both did. Someone was in the house, moving around. Sounded like a cat getting into the cereal boxes. But there were no cats at Dog House.

"Shit, it's her," he whispered.

"Who?"

"Avi's daughter. She lets herself in from the beach. Probably using the shower."

"The bitch?"

"Yeah."

"Are you fucking her?"

"Of course not, but if she catches you in here, I'll be out on the street. She thinks I'm trading close-ups for blow jobs."

"Well, *duh.*"

He got up, slipped into his Jams, gave her the shush signal. Giggling, she burrowed under the covers, popped back up, stuck her pierced tongue out at him. Like a magician, she was now holding and filling a tiny pipe with weed.

"Let me just get rid of her," Troy said.

He shuffled out barefooted, fixed his tousle of hair. "Zee? That you?"

He heard nothing, turned the corner and yelled. So did the aging Chinese guy in tinted glasses standing in the hall.

"Can I help you?" Troy said.

"You are Troy?"

"Who are you?"

"Your name is Troy?"

"Yes."

The Chinese guy shrugged innocently, then moved with deceptive quickness, laying a palm at Troy's chest and driving him across the room, against the wall. He felt like he'd been hit by a heavy, breaking wave. "What the *fuck*, man?"

"Pay boss."

"What?"

"Pay boss or I come back and break your legs."

In the bedroom, Alexis heard the confrontation, hid under the covers for a moment, then sat bolt upright. Hearing the scuffle, she dropped her tiny pipe and grabbed for her cell, quickly dialed 911, and whispered, "Somebody's fucking attacking my boyfriend. In his house. I don't know the address. Las Flores Beach in Malibu, east of Duke's. It's the brown house next door to Gary Busey's."

Out in the living room, Louie kept an iron-like finger high on Troy's chest.

"You understand me?"

29

"Who are you?"

"Never mind," Louie said, spittle flying. "Big trouble, you don't pay boss."

Louie turned on his heel, hurried toward the door. It was done. Over.

"Wait," Troy said, and Louie stopped. For a moment, panic danced across his eyes, swollen behind the amber tint of his glasses.

"Do I know you?" the kid said.

"What?"

Troy studied the face, knew he'd seen it somewhere. The loose jowls, thick head of black hair going gray, outsized sunglasses almost hiding a scar near the temple.

"No, you don't know me," the guy said.

"No, I think I do."

Louie went a shade of alabaster. Troy erupted into a sound that made Louie flinch. "Holy *shit. I know* you."

Louie fumbled for the door handle.

"*No Wires, No Nets,*" Troy blurted. "Am I right? The documentary. I watch it, like, once a month. You're Mo Chen Liu, the stunt guy. Am I right?"

Louie threw a befuddled look Troy's way. The damn antique brass door handle didn't work, neither up nor down.

"Louie Mo, the stunt man. Shaw Brothers Studios."

"You are crazy."

"*Shaolin Executioner. Five Deadly Venoms.* You did the full-burn scene on the boat in *City on Flame.*"

Louie turned again. From this well-lit angle, Troy was almost positive now.

"Louie Mo, right?"

"I don't know what you mean."

"What are you doing here? Are you working with Avi or something? Are you on a movie with Avi?"

"How do you know all this Hong Kong movie?"

"Victor Lo tried to say he did his own stunts in *Two Tigers of WuDang,* but you did them all. Except for that big roll down the temple steps, I think that was Victor."

"Bullshit," Louie spat, then caught himself. Maybe, he reasoned, he was still napping in the passenger seat and this was some crazy wine-and-oxy dream.

"Wait a minute," Troy said. "Did you say . . . did you say you were going to *break my legs*?" He laughed, incredulous.

"I'm not here."

"You're not here?"

"No, I'm here, but I'm not Louie Mo."

"You're not?"

Louie searched for an alternate escape, breezed quickly toward the French doors. "Wait," Troy interjected. "Can I just give you something?"

"No. What you give to me? You don't even know me. Just pay boss and let me go."

• • •

Out in the car, Dutch woke from a hazy nap. Sirens were whining closer. Two LAPD cruisers passed her, heading north then "flipping a bitch" as they say in the stunt world, swinging a wide U-turn and pulling in, one behind her, one forced to park on the highway. Lights were turning and it

31

made her cortisol spike. When she saw two cops walking toward the same brown house that Louie had entered, she did the thing that meant she was ready for lockup. She slipped off her right shoe, freeing her bare foot and her ankle bracelet, the one with a tiny St. Christopher medal on it. Monkey foot was what she called her driving style, a closer connection between driver and pedal. Her hand edged deliberately to the ignition. "Fuck a duck," she whispered.

• • •

"Would you read it?" Troy said.

Louie looked at the slim script in the kid's hands then glanced over his shoulder at the sound of sirens outside.

"It's called *The Cage*," Troy said. "A onetime famous cage fighter who killed a guy in an illegal match down in Mexico. He gets out of jail after twenty years. Tries to find his family and live a normal life, but the brothers of the guy he killed hear that he's out. They come after him."

"You make movie?"

"Everyone is after him. All the young guys in MMA, all different styles of fighting. It's like John Woo meets fifties Western noir meets *Run, Lola, Run*. It's kick-ass, Louie, almost like one big shot that doesn't let up. How cool would it be, Louie Mo in his first leading role? All his own stunts, not for someone else."

"You're crazy."

"I can pay you."

"What do you mean?"

"I've got some cash from the production I'm on now. I

can get you ten grand up front. Maybe another ten to finish and then some back end. Same as we just did for Eddie Morales on *Slash*."

Louie stared, incredulous. Twenty grand to star in an action movie, not just doing stunts? He looked around the big living room, did a quick inventory of shabby-chic furniture and framed art. This was Malibu, maybe this kid was for real. Louie was taking in the seven-million-dollar ocean view when he saw the cop at the open porch door, hand on his leather holster. A second cop sidled calmly alongside the house, same position.

"Shit," Troy said, "chick must've called the police."

When Troy started toward the cops, they calmly ordered him to stay where he was.

"Is there a problem here, bud?" the first cop said.

"No, Officer. My girlfriend must've called."

The cops were looking at the Asian man now.

"This is Louie Mo," Troy said, almost bragging. "Hong Kong stuntman. Legend."

When the cops angled unimpressed looks, Louie gave a slight nod.

"We got excited, about a script," Troy said. "That's all. There's no problem, Officer."

"Must be one hell of a script, bud," the first cop said, "if your girlfriend calls nine-one-one."

When the second cop saw Alexis peering out, he stared, expressionless. "Did you report an incident, Miss?"

"I thought," Alexis said, "this guy was assaulting my boyfriend."

The second cop scanned her through his Ray-Bans. "You from Charlie's house?"

"Yeah."

"I thought so."

"You the home owner?" the first cop asked Troy.

"No. Avi Ghazaryan the film producer owns the house. I'm the tenant."

The cops stayed on the porch for a moment, instructing Troy and Louie to stick around. Troy could tell that they were bored by the affair but were seizing the opportunity to loiter on a sunny Malibu balcony and catch a break from the freeway. After a few radio calls, they asked Troy again if there was a problem. Finally assured, they left.

Alexis, wearing nothing but Troy's violet NYU tee and her Uggs, eased out into the room a wary step. "Troy, what's going on?"

Troy ignored her, fixated again on Louie Mo. "Would you just think about it? We'd shoot the whole thing right here in L.A. in four weeks. I'll cut my fee if you need more money."

"Your name is Troy?"

"Troy Raskin. I had a film at Austin last year."

"You make a very big mistake, Troy. I work for a man who collects money for people. I came here to tell you only to pay your bills."

Louie left Troy in the hall, confused. Alexis hadn't moved either. "Troy, what the fuck is going on?"

· · ·

Out in the Chevy, Dutch felt a kind of vertigo as she drove. "He *knew* you?"

"I don't know how; nobody knows me. Always I'm behind the action."

"Is this a joke?"

"He know so much. Every movie. Every fight. Chinese names. Even my real Chinese name."

"*I* don't even know your real Chinese name. What's that in your hand?"

"Script."

"*What?*"

"He give to me. *The Cage.* Wants Louie Mo. Not just fighting. Star, twenty thousand dollars."

Dutch pulled over just before the overpass. She had her iPhone, double-thumbing. She grabbed the Jack in the Box napkin and Googled the name Troy Raskin and the word "movies." Halfway down the screen, she began to read:

"Troy David Raskin. NYU whiz kid wins Special Jury Mention at Austin Film Fest with offbeat heist drama."

"See? Believe me now?"

"NYU whiz kid," she said again. "Film school dude. Maybe he *does* know who you were."

"Knows more Chinese movie than me."

"Did he really say twenty grand? Don't fuck around, Louie."

"Cut his own fee, he said. If I do movie."

"Louie, this is insane."

"I know."

"You go in there to kick him in the balls and he offers you a movie deal?"

"I know."

She stared at him for so long, he wanted to shake her. Then she heard her phone chime a text. "Shit, we've got a taker on the football," she said, scrolling. "Baseball card dealer in Thousand Oaks."

She shifted into drive. Louie held the script like he was holding rare porcelain. He thumbed through it, not reading, just thumbing. He could tell, already, it was good. It felt good in his hands. Light. Not heavy like *Once Upon a Time in China 2*. That one took two years of his life and ruptured his spleen. And still, no one knew his name.

No one but that kid Troy on Las Flores Beach.

6

HERE COMES JESUS

The jaundiced guy with the sideburns and gauze taped across his damaged nose stood on the deck of Banazak's forlorn yacht, watching the ex-footballer rinse out a cooler. Coastal wind teased his thinning hair. "I'd never do anything to hurt you, J-Zak," he said.

Banazak didn't look at him. "What were you doing in the hotel room with these dirtbags selling my shit?"

"I was there trying to buy your stuff back. This fucking Chinese dude barges in and goes Bruce Lee on everyone."

"You were my agent, Tommy. Longer than Chasman was."

"I'm just in there, getting close to a deal. The guy hits me in the face. He grabs the jersey and the football and runs out. I had nothing to do with it. I just want you to know, man, I was there trying to buy back your stuff."

Banazak stared at him with those flat, dead eyes. "What did you say?"

"I was just there trying to buy back your shit."

"No, about the Chinaman. He took the jersey and the what?"

"The football. The game ball from the Super Bowl. It was on a stand, but he left that, just took the ball."

"He delivered the jersey. I've got that back. He didn't bring no ball. He said he couldn't find it."

"Oh, he found it. Had it under his arm when he was walking out. I remember because . . . the stupidest thing went through my head while I was lying there, my nose busted, covered in spaghetti. I thought: He's not protecting the rock. He can get stripped. Fumble waiting to happen."

Tommy laughed, but he was a nose-laugher and the snorting hurt his busted cartilage. "Stupid things that go through your head, you know, in the moment."

"He didn't deliver no rock."

"Check the security tape. They'll show you," Tommy said.

"The guy is going down the hall with the jersey under one arm and the football in the other."

Banazak's pupils dilated. He breathed in salt air, listened to chinkling boat chimes and gulls scavenging over near the Cheesecake Factory. "The jersey's a jersey. I ripped a dozen of them, gave a dozen to little kids. But that rock, man. That was a tipped ball at the line of scrimmage in the red zone. My big, lumbering ass took that ball eighty-seven yards to pay dirt. On national TV. My father fucking cried. Only game ball I was ever awarded. My whole career is in that ball."

"Yeah, well. Now some Chinaman probably has it on eBay."

DOG BEACH

Banazak kicked the cooler. The cover split a hinge, the tank slid off the boat into a slick of motor oil. "Here comes Jesus," he said, and he went down into the galley. The hair bristled on Tommy's nape. Those words. That's what J-Zak used to say aloud when he broke through the line and went after a quarterback with intent to kill. "Here comes Jesus."

Opposing linemen were said to void their bowels when they heard those words. Because few quarterbacks ever played another game; some never walked again.

Monterey Park would see the white girl in the Chevy come to pick him up, they never asked about it.

For the past two days he'd been resting his hip at the communal house, eating the old woman's soup, reading Troy's script, and taking solace in the fact that he made two grand in a matter of days. Half came from selling the "superball" to a dealer in Thousand Oaks, half from the elbow he put on the kid Troy in Malibu. Of course, he split the fee on both with Dutch. After paying Mother Celery for room and board he had a little more than nine hundred dollars inside the backpack that contained everything he owned: a red sweat suit, a pair of ostrich-skin loafers, a shaving kit, his passport, and several changes of socks and underwear.

Sometimes he felt like one of the Chinese emigrants who came to America to work on the railroad. Living day to day, paycheck to paycheck. A "coolie," Dutch told him they were called. One day Mother Celery set down his rice and said, in Cantonese, "Man with secrets. Who do you hide from?"

"Two ex-wives," he confided. "But you know, Grandmother, they have pills for female problems."

The old woman frowned then said in throaty Cantonese, "A man doesn't hide the way you do when he's just running from women who want his money."

Louie changed the subject, plying her with so many compliments about her soup that she eventually smile' with her termite's den of teeth, ladled him more, and let' conversation die. But it had troubled him. There were when he'd almost forgotten he was a wanted man ;

7

FIRE IN THE HOLE

Down between Garfield and Garvey, in the area known as Downtown Monterey Park, Louie Mo sat inside a crowded little house, speaking Cantonese to an old woman named Mother Celery. The English translations that some Chinese chose for their names forever baffled him. "Louie" was transnational, but "Celery"? Still, he wasn't going to tell Mother Celery that. The house was full of Chinese laborers, the surrounding area boasting the largest concentration of Chinese in any municipality in the United States. That's why he lived there. He could hide. Blend in. Relax, almost.

On the days or nights he went to work for his "agent," a Czech loan shark he called Boss Jim, he'd come back to the house tired and sleep in a room he shared with four other Chinese men. When they sat about and spoke Cantonese, Louie would tell them he washed dishes in South San Gabriel, didn't say much more. When the Chinese people of

Kong. But the kid Troy had disturbed him and he wondered again if this was now some kind of clever trap. Could the kid be a plant? Even the story line of the kid's script seemed to be a subtle threat: A character trying to find peace but hunted down by men from his violent past. Then again, if this kid was, like Dutch said, a walking database of kung fu movies, it wouldn't be unusual to write something like that—a silly white boy's notion of a cool Hong Kong flick.

Louie struggled with the English prose in the script, but the dialogue read cleanly. There wasn't much, except for a big speech right where the script dead-ended, unfinished. Some monologue about "the cages we build around ourselves." It sounded ridiculous, not the way real people talked. But who cared? Twenty thousand dollars was a winning lottery ticket right now. Shoot the movie in four weeks, tuck away the cash, and maybe go with Dutch to Las Vegas.

Louie was trying to read through that monologue now, but the Cantonese around him was getting too heated. Some drama was unfolding outside, some chatter about a little girl and her bicycle chain. No one could fix it. She blamed her little brother and bit him; he was wailing in the kitchen.

Finally, Louie slipped the script into the net pocket on his rucksack and lugged it with him outside. He entered the near hilarious circle around the girl's bike and he took a knee, saying nothing. As a stuntman on low-budget Hong Kong films, Louie had done it all. He'd rigged explosives, hung cable, chambered squibs, and even saddled horses. Fixing a little girl's bicycle chain was easy. When he looked up and saw her smiling through dried tears, he felt something he had become distant from. Pride. Just a hint, maybe, but it felt good.

That's when he saw the SUV.

Twice it had driven by, like a shark slowly cruising the shallows. It made a third round now, a bit more slowly. For Louie Mo, assessing danger was something of a handicap. He never knew quite how to describe it, but he once told Dutch that the brain chemicals normally triggered by fear had been so depleted by his years of high-falls and full-burns that he now had to draw on reason more than instinct. When he saw the gun in that man's hand back in the Palm Springs hotel room, it spiked no adrenaline. Yet, random and benign happenings could chill him to the core, make him break out in a sweat, like that talking E-Trade baby on the TV commercials. So now, watching that SUV circle the boardinghouse in an ever-tightening spiral, Louie drew on hard logic: Fire in the hole. Be alert.

He wasn't even back to the porch when he heard gravel crunching under fat, heavy tires. Two black men were in the backseat of the SUV. Riding passenger: a young white guy with a shaved head and an earring. But it was the man behind the wheel who looked dreadfully familiar.

The former football pro from Marina del Rey was wearing a silver-and-black Polo shirt, his meaty, tattooed arm hooked over the open window. The tiny wire-rimmed glasses he wore for driving offset the ferocious air. Until he took them off. He was out of the car now, gigantic. So were the two black guys, while the young whitey in the passenger seat was left behind to watch the vehicle.

Louie stood up, slowly. The steroid giant was walking straight toward the circle of Chinese as the little girl wobbled away on her repaired bike. Louie turned on his sneakers and walked casually, but quickly, back to the house.

"Hey," he heard the big man say. "I want to talk to you."

Louie entered the house, closed the door. Took a breath. Then he jogged. He jogged the length of the hall, his gaze fixed on the back door, the light outside. In seconds though, one of the black men was standing there, crouching to look in. Quickly, he let himself inside and said, "Yo, Grasshopper."

Louie turned abruptly, entered a bedroom full of girls. They looked up, silently, but when he stepped up onto a bed and opened a window, they screamed. He laid a finger alongside his nose, urging silence. They screamed louder, huddling in a corner. *Crazy fucking Chinese girls*, he groaned to himself.

Outside, he landed on his feet, like a cat on gravel. Then he winced. The hip, his elbow, the aging titanium screws in his lower back—all protested in one cruel spasm. But he had to run anyway, out toward the train tracks and the cluttered industrial area behind.

In the drainage alley, he saw him. The big *laowai*. The two colored guys had gone around one side, Banazak the other. He had a direct path to Louie Mo. Smiling, his face flushed, he started toward him. Louie's adrenaline kicked in:

In the narrow alley between two crappy houses, he can run between, split the gap. Instead, he runs straight ahead for the opposite wall. Cheating gravity, he runs up the cement

45

and siding. Not all the way up for a reverse somersault, just a few feet up so he can launch sideways, fire a hook kick. It hits Banazak in the ribs, throws him off course and into a stumble.

Somehow the big laowai *corrects the stumble, uses his momentum to twist and grab Louie, slam him against the cement. Louie tries to spin; Banazak comes in low and inside, pummels him like a hanging side of beef. Louie doesn't know what the hell is happening; feels like he's lost a step. But on the fourth punch, Louie traps it. The hard, powerful slap downward—*pak sao *in Cantonese—not only clears the big man's fist, it jerks him forward and low. Louie hits with a vertical fist. Then another. Then a half dozen, all in a blistering chain of vertical blows. An average man would crumple. Not Banazak. He rocks back two wounded steps, covers up like a boxer. "I'LL FUCKING KILL YOU," the steroid giant barks as Louie runs for daylight then side-shuttles onto a fire escape, goes upward. All the while, his backpack miraculously rides one shoulder.*

Over the rooftops, Louie Mo runs. He can see the tracks and wishes that, like in a movie, the train would come at the perfect time and he could jump onto it, ride away. But there's no train, no first AD directing him in an ear speaker, just a brutal jump down to dead tracks and scattered paper trash. How the black guys got onto the roof so fast, he can't figure. But when he sees how they move, he can tell: athletes. "GRASSHOPPER BOY," one of them yells. Louie has no idea why he keeps calling him "grasshopper" but he assumes, in the rush of the moment, that it's a black guy thing.

They come at him, one on each side. One is in a tae kwon do stance and appears capable. Very capable. The other has a gun coming out of a waistband, and he's yelling like a cop for Louie to get on the ground. Banazak is on the roof now, breathing like a winded, wounded water buffalo. He and Louie lock eyes. The big laowai *catches his breath, says something about Jesus.*

He doesn't charge, he rampages. Yelling. Blitzing. His eyes almost roll back in his head. Louie cyclones, back fists the brother with the gun, drops low and shin-rakes the second one. From his position on the ground, he rolls. It's the roll that a stuntman hopes will put out a full-burn if the fire extinguishers aren't doing the job. He rolls right off the roof. This time, he doesn't land like a cat. . . .

• • •

Flat on his back, he felt the wind huff from him, felt an odd tremor, wondered if he was having a kidney spasm. Not so. As Louie's bad luck would have it, a train *was* coming. He got up, started running, like a limping deer, west down the track. A horn-siren blared behind him, getting closer; air brakes were whooshing and screaming. Louie jumped onto the chain-link fence that kept kids off the tracks, crawled upward, clinging, letting the train thunder past. He could feel its power, its hydraulic wind ripping at his baggy jeans. His left hand was growing numb, falling asleep from clinging so hard to the fence.

From the rooftop, Banazak watched, gathering his

breath. When the train passed, Louie Mo was gone. Not a sign of him.

"Who *is* that motherfucker?" the brother with the gun said, laughing. If he didn't laugh, he'd feel bested.

"Dead," Banazak said, hands on his knees, sucking air. "A *dead* motherfucker."

8

THE DOGS OF ENTROPY

Troy was doing his barefoot run up the beach, earbuds in, trying to outpace his worries. It wasn't working. He'd been half-joking when he told his boys that they were hostages at Avi's beach house, but now the description felt all too apt. Maybe, somewhere in the back of his mind, he knew that he was making a Faustian deal with the B-movie producer, blinded by the allure of a Go pic, a six-figure budget, and sweet digs in Malibu.

He picked up his speed, lengthened his stride. *Dude, what were you thinking?* he huffed to himself. As always, though, he knew the answer, knew damn well what he'd been thinking: His student heist film had shown great promise and got some national press, but it was still a student film. *Slash* was going to get real distribution, Avi promised. Probably play for a solid week at the multiplexes, including back home in Fairfield County, Connecticut. He had rationalized the commitment as a stepping-stone toward making bigger and better movies, but he knew in his gut what was really behind it.

Success is the best revenge.

Some guys just fade away from the hometown that has mocked their ambitions; others fold and become a part of the local walking dead, join the naysayers in crushing those who dare to dream. Troy wanted to show them—the relatives, the classmates, the old girlfriends—that they were wrong not to bet on him. Wanted to show them that faith and hard work could move mountains, make movies. But it was all back-firing on him. The movie was a train wreck, his time was running out, and he already used a portion of the budget to make late payments on his Mini-Cooper. Now a displaced Hong Kong stuntman shows up at Dog House and threatens to break his legs?

Could it get any worse? Or, as Troy kept asking the boys, *could it get any better*? Troy had talked of little else since the strange encounter; *"Fucking Louie Mo,"* he'd kept ranting, running down the list of Golden Harvest movies the guy had a hand in. How bizarre was it that he'd walked out into the sun-drenched living room to find the dude standing there, eleven in the morning—and then the guy had put him up against the wall. The Dogs didn't find it all that strange; Avi's house drew all kinds.

Durbin had said something else then too. Having come out of the USC screenwriting program, the young writer had something of an unhealthy obsession with the Hero's Journey structure. "Have you ever considered," he told Troy, "that this dude who showed up at the house is like some fucked-up version of the Supernatural Aide? Like Obi-Wan Kenobi. Or Gandalf."

"Maybe," said T-Rich. "But he could just as easily be the Evil Guardian of the Threshold. He did threaten you with violence."

Avi must have hired him through his big-money connections, Troy reasoned. The behind-the-scenes engine they didn't teach you about in film school. Life was unscripted on Dog Beach, bro; anything could happen. That's what Troy told Durbin then and it's what he was thinking now as he jogged past celebrity homes. He slowed down to eye a certain duplex and take a beat to catch his breath. It was the beach house where Timothy Treadwell had once been a boarder and so it held a strange fascination for Troy. Zoe had told him that the Treadwell kid used to sit on the porch and wait endlessly for dolphins. Whenever a school would appear, the kid would fly off the porch and begin making high-frequency wails, running in the surf with his left elbow folded behind his back, emulating a fin. Sometimes Dolphin Boy would get overwhelmed and swim out to them, assigning them names. The point of the anecdote, said Zoe, was that Dolphin Boy decided to move to Alaska and explore the same bonding relationship with grizzlies. He gave them names like Quincy and Emmy and Mr. Chocolate. One autumn day they ate him. That was how Dolphin Boy became Grizzly Man, the subject of the Werner Herzog film.

Life was unscripted. Alaska was not Safari World and Hollywood was not Disneyland; there were no rails to keep you from falling into the dark if you made a pact with the

51

wrong guy for the wrong reasons. Troy had to get out of this mess somehow, or everything he had ever dreamed of would go out to sea with the sewage.

Just past Matthew McConaughey's place, he turned around, his shoulders to the sun. He began jogging the two miles back to Dog House, wondering if it was too early for a beer.

• • •

On a scale of one to ten, the getaway from the Palm Springs Marriott had ranked a soft five. This Dutch Dupree judged by how long the odd euphoria lasted, how long she'd completely forgotten what depression felt like, how long she'd gone without feeling the need for another jolt of pure cortisol.

She was parked at the curb of the Laurel Canyon house where she'd been staying with Crazy Jen, a makeup artist she met on a movie set in Santa Fe. The neighborhood was quiet during the day and she sat there for a time, reflecting on the past forty-eight hours, her latest gag with Louie Mo. Maybe it ranked a six; she had even slept well last night, parked in the Marina harbor.

"Hey, girl," Jen said when Dutch came through the door. She said it without looking away from an up-do she was sculpting on some dark chick, the two laughing in silly delirium as they drank margaritas. Los Lonely Boys was blasting from an iPod deck.

Dutch stared at the drinks for a moment too long; it almost made her want one. So she made it a point to glide quickly past her roommate and receive an intercepting smooch from Charles, the petite Romanian hair stylist who lived there on and off. Dancing overtly to the Texican rock, Charles spun off the kiss, did a Zumba move, and said, "How's my little speed racer?"

Oh, he added, as she made her way to the shower, he had a lead on a job for her, a legal gig on an independent film shooting up in Fresno. They needed a stuntgirl who could ride a Ninja sport bike up a flight of stairs.

"Regrettably, I pass," Dutch said, getting out of her hoody and jeans, bathroom door open. It didn't matter that Charles was standing there, watching her undress. She wasn't his type.

"What do you mean you pass? Nobody passes, not in this economy."

"Not available," she said.

"It's nonunion. They won't run a background check. I already asked." Then Charles crimped his nose: "My God, you smell like an ashtray; let me toss these in with my wash."

Charles gathered up her clothes, then averted his eyes as he held out a hand, as regal as a stage prince, for her panties. She smiled and hesitated. "If I knew you were going to undress me, I wouldn't have worn the beige ones."

She stripped them off boyishly, and he kept his eyes politely away. She stole her jeans back for a quick moment, removed a pill vial and a scrunched twenty from a pocket. "You can't keep doing this, Dutch," said Charles.

"Doing what?"

"Driving a getaway car. For you-know-who. Your Korean hit man or whatever."

"He's Chinese."

53

"I don't care if he's the King of Siam, you're going to get yourself arrested. Or worse."

Dutch laughed, if such a cynical hiss could be called laughter. How she'd come to board at the Laurel Canyon house was common in the circus-troupe world of film crews. She had been working on a Western when she bruised her thigh purple and Jen the makeup artist covered it in concealer so Dutch could wear her Daisy Duke cutoffs to the wrap party at the Pink Adobe. Now Jen rented her the back room of her rented L.A. house, a crash pad for the hair-and-makeup fraternity. A strange lair for a stuntgirl but a room just the same.

As she surrendered her beige undies to Charles, he turned and looked at her full-on over the rims of his red designer glasses. She was naked but for her ankle bracelet, and too tired to care. Charles clucked his tongue.

"Why don't you let Jen do something about those bags under your eyes? You look like fucking Al Pacino."

Dutch lightly ushered Charles out, closed the door.

"At least ice them," he sang from the other side of the door as she turned on the warm water and stepped in to rinse away four days on the dusty road. The economy had nothing to do with it. Riding a sport bike up a flight of stairs just didn't cut it anymore. If adrenaline was alcohol, that kind of stunt was soda pop.

Her long hair, almost dreadlocked by a few days of wind and neglect, wasn't even wet in the shower when her cell rang. Louie Mo. She reached from the stall, grabbed it, squeezed into a dry corner.

"What's up?"

He had to say it over the roaring echo of some freeway somewhere. "Big trouble."

• • •

HOW TO MAKE MOVIE BLOOD

Gather the following ingredients:

- 1 *level tsp. zinc oxide*
  (any laboratory supply)

- 1 *oz. red food color*

- 1 *oz. yellow food color*

- 1 *quart white corn syrup*

- 1 *oz. Kodak Photo-Flo *Poisonous**
  (any photo supply store)

- 1 *oz. water*

1. Put the zinc oxide and Photo-Flo into a bowl, add an equal amount of water and paste. Add the food coloring and stir.

2. Add a little of the corn syrup and mix well. Pour into a container that holds more than the final amount (you have to shake it up before use, as it may separate), add the remaining corn syrup and mix well. Then add the amount of

water specified and mix again. This will give your blood a normal consistency. Keep this and all corn syrup recipes refrigerated when not in use (or it will grow mold) and mix well before use.

WARNING: Due to one of the ingredients being poisonous, this blood recipe should not be used if it is likely to be swallowed during or after application—that is, of course, unless you want a real death in your movie.

3. Malone's Exploding Squib Technique:

Pour mixture into ultra-thin latex condoms, tie off condoms, and drape each over weight-lifting belt. Hide belt under clothing. *KA-BOOM*. Actor slaps at torso, blood explodes.

This Malone was experimenting with at the kitchen table—his own twist on makeup legend Dick Smith's recipe—when the door buzzer sounded. He had been smoking weed while making his mixture, so he sat paranoid for a moment before cleaning his hands and making his barefoot way down the hall.

"Yeah, I got it," he said when Troy called out from his bedroom.

Whoever was ringing the beach house's doorbell was not announcing themselves, but Malone, high on weed, just kept asking, "Who is it?" After a fourth ring, the ginger scratched his temple, shrugged, and walked away. The voice came over the speaker then, hoarse tones of broken English:

"Me. Louie Mo."

Troy came flying around the corner in his running shorts, wet towel in his grip. Within seconds, Louie Mo was inside, this time accompanied by a dangerous-looking girl with a tiny nose ruby and a tattoo on her shoulder that read "Radar Love." On her left wrist, three Indian horse-hair bracelets were loosely ringed.

"Driver," Louie said, gesturing toward the girl.

"You must be Troy," she said.

"Come on in." Troy's voice was thin with excitement, still a little winded from his jog. Durbin met them too. Then T-Rich and Malone, hiking up his baggy plaids. "*Mahalo*," he said.

"Can I get you guys a beer?" Troy said.

Moments later they were sitting around the living room, drinking chilled Coronas, all but Dutch, who took ice water instead and played the role of interpreter. She told Troy that Louie had indeed been sent to the house earlier at the request of an unnamed employer; he'd been doing a little moonlighting as a bill collector. He wanted Troy to know, she explained, that it was nothing personal, that he considered that uncomfortable piece of business behind them now.

"So who sent him? Avi?"

Louie shrugged, and Dutch said, "Never heard that name. Louie's jobs are all outsourced through one guy, and it doesn't matter now."

Malone considered the bill collecting and said, "Would this have anything to do with outstanding student loans?"

No one answered him, but he was used to that.

"Bottom line," Dutch said, keeping with her translator tone. "Louie loves your script."

"Sweet."

"He wants to do it."

Troy was leaning forward in his chair, drumming a pencil on his knee and smiling in a way Durbin hadn't seen in thirteen months.

"Mr. Mo," Troy said. "This is unbelievable."

"You are very smart," Louie finally said. "Good script. But no ending."

"No, no, I know. I had to stop when I started the Avi movie."

"Where do you see it going?" Dutch said. She was drawn to the glass doors now, a silhouette against the ocean view.

"I don't know yet," Troy said. "Endings are always a bitch."

"Explosion," Louie said assuredly.

Troy started to laugh, thinking it a sarcastic joke about Hollywood depravity. Durbin grinned too, but then they saw that Louie was dead serious. Malone arced his red brow. "A man after my own heart," he said.

When the boys broke into their "Malone Zone" chant with sports-bar vigor, Louie smiled uncomfortably, looking to Dutch for perspective. Malone gave a thumbs-up and Troy explained that the kid was the effects talent in the house.

"Serial arsonist," joked T-Rich.

"Pyrotechnician," the redhead insisted.

"Big exploding," Louie kept on. "Me, I am running from the guys. Bad guys. What is my name again?"

"Cho," Troy said.

"Cho," Louie echoed, letting it sink in for a moment, like he was tasting and assessing some wine. "Cho running from guys in building. Ready to explode. I do the biggest jump ever for Louie Mo. No wires."

"Yeah, buddy," said Troy, leaning back and punching the air. Durbin fidgeted, uncertain. Malone just grinned, staring at the former stuntman with an almost morbid curiosity.

"I can do this," Louie said, removing his tinted Ray-Bans. "Sign contract, I do this. Biggest fucking Louie Mo jump ever. Bigger than Jackie. Jet. No kung fu bullshit. Real. People won't believe."

Troy paced, kept flinging excited glances at Durbin, and then Malone. "Well, that's kind of perfect," he said. "Cho gets trapped in a building," he said. "Caged."

"We can blow a condemned fire trap," said Malone. "A lot of L.A. 'hoods are eager to have a film company take one down for free."

"It's *The Cage*, man," said Troy, growing near feverish. "It's the metaphor. Nowhere left to run."

"Can you score those kind of fireworks?" Durbin asked Malone.

"I don't know, man. I can rig charges and shit, but I don't know where to get the big loads."

"I do," Dutch said. They all looked at her. She was standing there, contemplating the ice cubes in her empty glass, mumbling something about an effects guy over in Irvine.

Then she said, "You know your movies, Troy. You know your stunt drivers?"

"A few."

"Ever hear of Dutch Dupree? Drove a lot for Mickey Gilbert in the nineties."

"Precision?"

"Yeah. Only chick in the club. Dutch the Clutch."

"No, don't think I know that name. But I'm not that up on my stunt drivers."

"That's her," Louie said, cocking his head in the girl's direction. "Driver. Very good."

"Mostly out of Santa Fe," Dutch said. "I'm in between gags."

"Good," Louie underscored. "Good control. Fast."

"Nice," Troy said. "We could use that."

"Roll another five grand into Louie's fee, and you've got my wheel."

When Troy looked back to Louie, the legend was gone. Then he appeared again, coming out of one bedroom, looking into another; he was casing the place like a prospective buyer.

"I stay here?" Louie said. "While we make the Cage movie."

Troy looked at Durbin. "You guys have any issues with High Flying Louie Mo, Hong Kong stunt king, staying at Dog House?"

"Shit no," Durbin said. "That'd be sick."

The others shrugged or nodded, but no one contested.

"Friggin' Louie Mo, living with the Dogs," said Troy.

"Why you say Dogs?"

Louie was looking at Troy, suspicious, his eyes darting to his driver for some help.

"That's what we call our crew," Troy said. "The Dogs."

"The Dogs of Entropy," Malone explained. "It's kind of a loose production company, co-op, think-tank, garage-band kind of enterprise."

"Louie," Dutch said, the way one might speak to the hard of hearing. "They're not having you sleep with the dogs. They call themselves the Dogs."

When Troy laughed, Louie did too, even slapped his leg, but he still didn't get it, "dog" being a serious slur in China. Didn't really matter now. He felt a great opportunity here. Big money, big house. On the beach. Funny boys. Light hearts, cold beer. With lime wedges. Louie leaned back in the white shabby-chic chair, relaxing. But somewhere inside, he still felt unsettled as hell from the rooftop donnybrook.

Dutch said she had to go; Louie said he'd call her. As she headed out, both Troy and Durbin took note of her tattoo and ankle bracelet. And her well-made bottom. If she drove stunts in the '90s, she must've been a mere kid back then. At the door, she turned, tapped a cigarette loose and set it on her lip.

"Take good care of Louie Mo."

"He's the man," said Troy.

Louie liked that. He sank deeper into the overstuffed chair and looked out at blue sky and ocean. Troy caught a look from Dutch then, saw her taking in the full view of the nice house. There was something in her demeanor that unsettled him. Something dubious, maybe—what Malone would call "sketch." But Louie Mo's body of work spoke for itself, and when Troy turned back, he lowered his Corona to Louie's and clinked. "Old school," he said.

"Old school," Louie echoed back, but he didn't have a clue what it meant.

He was soon outside on the back porch, looking at the surf and the Las Flores Beach walkers while Troy and the boys downed more brews in celebration, never taking their eyes off him. Life is very strange, he thought to himself. You just never know. Yesterday, he was in a low-rent neighborhood in Monterey Park, convinced his miserable life was going to end there. Now, here he was in Malibu, in a fancy beach house, making a movie deal with Hollywood's new generation. Maybe, he mused, he had been meant to come to Southern California all along. . . .

• • •

It was 1993 when he left Hong Kong for good. His escape destination was a natural choice, a routine flight plan in the business: Vancouver. A thirteen-hour trip to another continent yet familiar enough to Louie that he could call on a favor, maybe find a gig.

On the plane, feeling safe and wishing he could just stay up there, he carefully dislodged business cards from his battered wallet. Some of the cards were so old they were faded and stuck together. One of them, the one he was hoping was still there, had a logo of an exploding car and the title: Sean King, Stunt Rigger.

DOG BEACH

Sean King was an Englishman based out of Vancouver. "You think English are sissy boys, all the time drinking tea?" Louie used to say in the days he worked with Sean. "Tough boys. Like to fight. Mean."

He did stunts up in Calgary twice with Sean's crew, but he couldn't remember the films now. Just a lot of wire work and free tumbles from cliffs, rock-climbing action. So he put Sean's card in a wallet pocket behind a photo of an infant girl and took a deep nap. When he got to Vancouver he would ring Sean, let him know he was available. Canada was a good place to work.

He checked into a crappy motel outside of Chinatown, not *in* Chinatown because those places made him anxious. Just close enough so he didn't stand out to anyone who might be looking for him, or bump into anyone who might recognize him. It took Sean a week to return his call.

"Sorry, man, I was in fucking Romania."

"Romania is good," Louie said. "I come work for you."

"We're about wrapped," Sean said. "I'm back in Vancouver in three weeks. Let's get together then and get jolly drunk."

"Jolly drunk is good," Louie said, and they made plans to meet up when the tough Englishman was back. Three weeks became four, then five, and Sean had still not called. That was normal in the biz. Most movies ran over schedule, especially second unit crews that had to go back and shoot pick-ups. So Louie didn't take it as a slap. He was low on money, though. His one credit card was now rejected, and he cashed in all his Chinese money to get a disturbingly thin wad of Canadian notes.

He had to take a job.

At a restaurant in Chinatown, a large, tacky place all red and gold called the Monkey King, he applied for a dishwashing job. The owner, a tiny Fujianese woman with a pretty face and angry scowl told him no, right then and there. He was standing at the bar while she mixed a vodka with lychee and stabbed a plastic umbrella into the froth.

"I don't like your face," she said.

Louie lingered while she glided off in her emerald silk to deliver the tropical drink. He walked out into the night and felt terrible. Not so much about being broke and out of work as he did about the woman's remark. *Mean lady,* he said to himself. He wanted to get jolly drunk, but didn't. He went back to the motel and looked at the newspaper ads again. A few calls later, he had an interview with some industrial painters. Two days later he was on scaffolds and ladders, painting buildings. The French brothers he worked for were nasty suckers, but he stayed quiet and soon earned their respect for his agility up on the scaffolds. They would gaze at him with a kind of bewildered amusement as he painted eaves with one foot on a ladder rung and the other suspended in the air, like Harold Lloyd in the silent *Safety Last!* But his painting skills were awful; he made an unholy mess of things, ruined a good pair of pants.

Still, he replenished his wallet, paid his rent. Had enough to eat. A month later, Sean King called him, said he had finally made it back to Vancouver. Some shit had gone down in Romania, he said; his crew hadn't been paid for the extra work, so he got caught up in politics and accounting

64

and finally collected a rucksack full of cash, under the table. Paid his boys off and came home.

Louie warmed to the story about getting paid in cash. Especially when it was delivered in rucksacks. Romania sounded ideal.

"Let's meet for a dram, mother," Sean said. Louie said he didn't have wheels, so Sean told him to name a place where they could grab a drink and talk shop.

"Monkey King," Louie said, not sure why he suggested the gaudy place that wouldn't hire him. It just seemed convenient and the only name he remembered.

At five that night, Sean King walked into the Chinese restaurant wearing his leather jacket and tennis shoes that made him light on his feet even as he limped like most stunt veterans. He hugged Louie, they laughed, then sat at the bar and ordered tall glasses of vodka, no ice.

65

Mean Lady turned from her cash register and squinted at Louie for a long moment. He gave her the sweetest smile he could muster and she curled her lip in disgust.

"Did you wrap the Mandarin Films gig?"

"Yeah. All done."

"You usually overlap, mate, you're never available."

"Tired of Hong Kong."

Sean sipped his vodka and studied Louie up close. He seemed to be able to read him, could tell something wasn't right. Sometimes a stunt gone bad could have that effect, turn a man dark for a while.

"TV series starting up in about two months," Sean finally said. "Cop show."

Louie looked at him with keen interest as Sean lit a cigarette, then lit one for Louie.

"No kung fu, though," Sean said. "Straight-up fighting. Cop shit."

"Cop shit, I like," Louie said.

"How's that knee, man?"

It was then that Louie's eyes picked up something in the mirror near where Mean Lady was straightening bottles of alcohol and little jars of umbrellas. A young Chinese man entered from the street, a beanie on his head, sunglasses, hands jammed into the pockets of a sleeveless jacket. One of his thin arms bore a tattoo that Louie couldn't make out. Behind him, three more teenagers followed, so closely they touched one another. Something both nervous and angry in their steps.

"The knee, Louie, you still getting those shots?"

Louie could see all four teens looking at him from behind. He could see Mean Lady turning slowly, then fully, as if she recognized the youths and didn't like their faces.

The guns came up at the same moment Louie's adrenaline surged. Bullets smashed the mirror and Mean Lady yelled. Deep, almost like a man. Sean went to the floor, shielding his head. Louie went over the bar, rolling, and launching himself toward the kitchen area door.

Mean Lady took a bullet in the forehead and was pitched back against the bar bottles. People were screaming from the tables. Louie passed through the kitchen, overtook a running chef and a dishwasher. Both men dove to the ground, thinking that Louie might be one of the shooters.

In the back parking lot, Louie kept running. He knew that Sean was all right. Only four shots had been fired. Three had hit the mirror and one had struck Mean Lady. Sean was savvy enough to stay low and still. A professional. Louie was certain of that.

So he didn't look behind him as he slowed his run to a casual jog and made his way to the motel. The phone in his room was ringing off the night table. Could be Sean, he thought, but could be trouble. People looking for him. Those Chinese youths were some kind of street gang, the kind that serves a bigger and badder organization.

Breathless, Louie sat on the edge of his unmade motel bed and listened to the phone ring. Maybe they were aiming for Mean Lady. Maybe she hadn't paid lucky money to a Chinatown street gang. Or maybe they had come in to off Louie, shoot him in the back while seated at the bar.

He had to get out of Vancouver.

Had to catch a bus because he couldn't afford another flight. Had to find somewhere else where he could get lost, yet still keep some tenuous hold on the only work he really knew how to do. When his doorknob moved and someone tried to get in, he sprung from the bed, moved to the tiny bathroom. But it was only housekeeping, a Mexican girl who never waited more than two knocks to unlock the door and enter. When she saw Louie, she began to apologize and leave.

"No, no, it's okay," he said.

He set two crimped and sweaty Canadian dollars on the bed, grabbed his duffel bag, and left the room. As he hurried his way to the Greyhound station, baseball cap and sunglasses on, he made a decision under pressure. He was hardwired to do that, still alive because of it.

Los Angeles. Hollywood. He knew people. Kind of. It's where he should have gone in the first place.

9

THE COFFEE BEAN

Avi Ghazaryan sat alone at an outside table at 8591 Sunset Plaza Drive. It was an overcast morning, a tad cool for late June. Although he rented office space at Lantana in Santa Monica, the place was making him nervous. Too many fly-by-night productions came and went, often coming in with money, going out broke and looking scared, just to hang their shingle at Lantana for six months and roll legit. Avi much preferred his table at the Coffee Bean and was seriously thinking about putting its Sunset Plaza address on his business card. He could say he had an office upstairs, but he preferred casual outdoor meetings.

It was a soothing ritual: The L.A. *Times* spread open under a double espresso and a script, his focus on his iPhone, scrolling the trades. But he was brooding today, still surly over Tyler at Paramount. It had taken a few days, but the WME boys had gotten him in to see the production prez. Tyler, he'd felt, screwed him again. The meeting itself felt

like a home run. At one point during the pitch, Tyler inter-
rupted and asked if the concept had any foreign value. Avi
had come prepared, leaned forward in his chair:

"Cross a street in London, there he is. In Germany he
wears a hat—they call him Ampelmännchen. In Mexico
City, he moves his feet. Taiwan? At every crossing you will
find him. What do you mean, 'foreign'? The guy is as inter-
national as fucking Robin Hood. Or Snow White."

Avi let the words sink in: Robin Hood. Snow White. In-
ternational. Home run. Grand slam, even. Yet in the eleva-
tor, going down, Avi had a nagging feeling. No sooner was
he out the door, he imagined, than Tyler turned to his D-girl
and had her call Sacco and Vanzetti or whatever their names
were, that young writing team barely out of braces that had
the Midas Touch of the month. He'd pitch *Caution* to those
eager little gamers as if it were his own idea, have them tag-
team a draft in a month's time. The business always had a
reptilian scent, but it was worse these days. At least reptiles
had blood in their veins, cold as it might be. This new breed
was robotic. Robotic cannibals, eating the scrap metal of
their comrades and crapping out homogenous product. How
badly he missed the old days when dirtbags had souls and
studio heads didn't have names like Tyler.

Scrolling Nikki Finke, Avi's mind went to his next fixa-
tion: Troy Raskin. Little motherfucker. The clock was tick-
ing. Avi needed a cut to show his nervous investors, especially
Hektor's L.A. crew from Little Guatemala; they were getting
antsy. He had paid a grand to Papagallo's guy and heard that
a "persuader" made a visit to Troy, gave him a real-world

warning. He'd see now if that had put a fire under his ass. Then Avi could put together a distribution deal, the fun stuff.

"Avi," a voice said. The guy who pulled up two chairs wasn't just fat, he was the kind of guy who got kicked off of planes for taking up a row of seats. He wore bling over a bright blue-and-black-striped tracksuit and a baseball hat turned backward, and he talked like a brother even though he looked Polish American. "Where's the movie, yo?"

Maybe Lantana was better, Avi mused. At least there was a security gate that could keep investors like Bobby Gronkowski out.

"Four weeks, my friend, I'll show you a cut," Avi said.

"Cool, bruh," said Gronkowski—who went by the faux 'hood name L'il G—working his stubby fingers in the wrapper of some kind of coffee cake. He claimed to carry a small heater in his waistband; Avi wondered if he was packing it now.

"'Cause that's music money, homes," L'il G said. "And I got to turn it right back into my payroll. You still gonna use my soundtrack, bruh?"

"At the end when the credits roll."

"And my name?"

"In the credits."

"At the beginning or at the end?"

"At the end. That's what people remember, walking out of the cinema, hearing your soundtrack and seeing your name."

"You're not blowing smoke up my ass, are you?"

Avi turned his eyes on L'il G, said nothing. He reached

inside his jacket and removed a checkbook case made of Tumi leather. L'il G fidgeted with his coffee cake as he watched Avi write a check. "What are you doing?"

"Giving you your money back."

"Why?"

"There are other recording artists looking to place a song in a hit movie. Trust me."

L'il G reached across the table and gestured for the producer to not be so rash. "Hey, man, I was just sayin'."

"In four weeks, I will show you a cut," Avi repeated.

L'il G tugged gently at the soul patch under his lip, thinking this through. Finally, he nodded and resumed his work on the coffee cake. Then he noted that someone else was standing there now, waiting for a moment with Avi. Alexis Cain gave the large man a repulsive look as he closed the meeting and navigated his bulk past her. Avi liked the way men were now darting their eyes between him and the girl's tramp stamp as she stooped to kiss him on the cheek.

"How are you, darling?" Avi said.

"All right, I guess," she said. "Whatever."

She sat and reached into her messenger bag, removed something small. Avi admired her blue fingernails as she slid the object across to him.

"That's his rough cut."

Avi gazed down at the flash drive then lifted his handsome eyes to the girl. "You are fantastic," he said.

Alexis looked down at the remains of the coffee cake the fat man left behind. "*Ew,*" she said, folding her freckled arms. "You getting me a meeting with Gersh?"

DOG BEACH

Avi smiled at her mercenary approach. He leaned back, poked at his iPhone, and sent a text. Then he set the phone down firmly as if to say "done."

A barista boy, cleaning the next table over, felt Avi gently take his elbow. "Would you please clean that fucking coffee cake off the table?"

Alexis smiled at Avi. She liked older, distinguished men in Fred Segal blazers. She liked watching him hold the little flash drive like it contained the trading secrets of Wall Street. She felt like a Bond girl. With a meeting at the Gersh Agency she believed she just might become one.

10

TORRANCE, WAREHOUSE DISTRICT

Troy and his small guerrilla crew hit the ground running. The first scene they would shoot was a waist-high single on Louie Mo, in the role of Cho the ex-con, walking across a barren lot, hands jammed deep in the pockets of a blue windbreaker he'd picked out of Troy's closet.

Creeping backward with his old-school Arri 435, Troy's baggy shorts bulged at the pockets with lenses, motors, and compressed air. As he picked up the "John Ford shot" hand-held and backlit, T-Rich caught the long shot in HD wide-angle from the second floor of an abandoned warehouse.

This would be part of the film's opening title sequence, Cho returning to the neighborhood where he once lived to find that things had changed. The voiceover that Louie would record later was along the noirish lines of, "After twenty years in the slammer, I was a free man, no longer in the cage. Not the prison in Mexico, nor the cage that put me there."

Louie would struggle with the word "slammer," so they switched to "jail" and finally to "the pen" with good results. Louie savored the opportunity to simply stroll across a lot, no running or jumping. No going up in a harness and getting stuck up there until lunch. Today, all he had to do was walk like James Dean, shoulders hunched against a slight breeze. He felt young again, empowered. So much so he tried not to smile in the shot.

"Nice, Louie," Troy said, after shooting more than four hours of the walking scene from various angles, tons of coverage. The sun was getting close to magic hour, and he wanted to close out the first day with some vintage Louie Mo. He rubbed his hands together, smiled at Dutch. She was sitting on the hood of the Chevy, dangling her feet and smoking a cigarette.

"What do you think? Ready to light it up?"

Dutch stubbed her cigarette, slid off the hood. "Box ninety?" she asked.

"Box ninety right into the lot. Hit your mark, Louie will roll over the hood. Come down and go right into the blow-for-blow with Matty. T-Rich will sit up front with you and shoot the reverse. Give me some twitchy cam, T."

"Like 24?"

"Fuck 24. I want *French Connection*."

"We're losing our light, dude."

"No worries," Troy told him. He'd just overcrank the camera and shoot at 8fps instead of 24fps, draw more light on the film.

"Want some smoke?" Malone champed from the sidelines, scooping some Pyrolite in a flour sifter.

"Not yet."

Matty Ng, a beefy young Thai, smiled from under his black hoody, his hands bound in filthy fighter's wraps. Troy had scouted him at a Muay Thai gym downtown and offered him a nice little purse to play one of the young MMA thugs trying to make their name by beating Cho. "You get to be in a fight scene with Louie Mo," Troy offered as a perk, but Matty had no idea who Louie Mo was; he just liked the idea of fighting in a movie, showing his girlfriend the check he got for it. Louie walked up to him now, and with just a nod, cued him to practice their fist exchange at slow speed. Troy watched, clearing his throat excitedly. This was pro stuff and Louie seemed in his element. But when Matty finished up the practice routine by faking with a knee, Louie shoved him backward. "No playing around on movie!"

The set went quiet. Matty recovered, took a cocky step toward the aging Chinese stuntman. "Yo, dude, easy."

"Safety first!" Louie yelled back.

"Okay, bro, got it."

"No joke!" Louie pressed a finger. "Time is money!"

Troy felt he better step in or Louie could go on with his union rules until after dark. "Let's roll, Louie."

On "action," Dutch sped down Western Avenue with the roaring, "controlled uncontrollability" of a precision driver. Wearing a skull cap as a double for a bad guy, she hit her

77

E-brake and executed a deep, long skid, carving a turn at a perfect ninety degrees as Louie ran into frame, hit metal with his knee, and pitched himself into a roll over the hood. Coming down on the other side, he was face-to-face with Matty Ng, mugging for the camera in his hoody and hand wraps. They fired their exchange at full speed, but when Matty lost track and tried to improvise with an elbow, Louie stepped on his front foot, entered, and knocked him out. Cold.

"Cut!" Troy yelled, hurrying over.

"Louie!" Dutch said, jumping out from behind the wheel.

"I thought maybe he block," Louie said kneeling over the Thai kid and checking his chin. "Hey. You. Okay?"

Matty stirred and rolled over, touching his eye socket. "Fuck you, man," he said. "That's not in the script."

"Elbow not in the script either," Louie countered.

Louie looked up at Troy. "You get the punch?"

"Yeah."

Louie winked. Troy smiled. T-Rich held up his HD camera to say he got a zoom angle on it too.

"Hong Kong fighting not for sissy," Louie said to Matty as he helped him up.

• • •

Back at Dog House, Troy sat at his MacBook, earbuds in, writing into the night like he hadn't done in a year. The day had fueled him, fired his passion again, and he was on a third-act rampage. Louie was right, he decided: The surviving bad guys would trap the beleaguered Cho in an old building, planning to blow it sky high. (Troy made a margin note: *Check with Malone about rigging demolition charges.*)

In the final minutes of the movie, Louie Mo would time his most spectacular stunt of all time and jump, with no wires, from the building to the dinosaurian neck of a construction crane just as a bitch-load of controlled explosives blew out the top floor of the condemned structure, a fire trap they scouted in a bankrupt city north of Chinatown, toward Pasadena. (*Check with the city and fire department.*) Louie would then ride the steel cable downward and finish off his opponents in a smash-mouth sequence (NOTE: *tight, claustrophobic, real-world shit*) intercut with flashbacks from the illegal cage fight that ruined his life. The movie would end with Louie walking alone across the desert outside Las Vegas, toward an uncertain future, like a gunfighter who'd outlived his era.

Troy was so immersed in the scene that he forgot he said he'd meet his housemates for beers in Venice. Nor did he hear Zoe come in, her heels clicking, Prius keys landing on the countertop. "Hey, writer boy," she said. "Working on my scene?"

Troy turned, yanking at his earbuds. "Hey, Zee."

Zoe crossed the kitchen, went into the bathroom—and screamed. Louie Mo was sitting on the toilet thumbing idly through *PC Gamer* magazine. He covered himself and said, "Hello, I'm sorry," in Cantonese.

Troy sprung up, wheeled to meet her. "There's a Japanese guy on the bowl," she said, grabbing her keys in escape mode.

"That's Louie Mo," Troy said. "He's my new stunt co-ordinator."

"Jesus," Zoe said, calming herself. When Louie came out, she was somewhat polite and apologetic. So was Louie, and she noticed his limp.

"Troy, can I talk with you?" she said, cocking her head slightly toward the dark hall.

In the bedroom, Troy latched the door, turned to face her. She was staring at his unmade bed, script pages scattered about.

"Everything okay?" Troy said.

Zoe pushed him over, awkwardly, onto the bed. With one quick zip of her tiny mocha-colored dress, she was naked, peeling it off over her strappy high-heeled sandals. Her body, lethally posed, nearly sent him into the kind of asthma attack he used to have in high school. "I want my character to kill the redhead," she said, pulling a pin from her hair and letting it fall.

"Say again?"

"My character, Troy. She kills fucking Alexis with a nine-millimeter."

Troy stared at her for a beat. "Alexis plays a zombie. She's undead. She's supposed to kill *you* at the end."

"Whatever that bitch did to get that role, I can do better."

"Jesus."

• • •

Louie Mo was trying to get upstairs to the little bedroom that faced the ocean. He had been going up and down those stairs quite easily, but tonight, after a long day of shooting, it was an effort. Less than halfway up, he felt himself sweating from the pain. The moderate gag he had done was nothing compared to his lifetime of daredevil achievements; most of the shoot was of him walking across the empty lot like a sullen antihero. But the shoulder roll across the hood of the Chevy did a number on his hip. The knee was fine, never an issue, really. In fact, he had done some of the wilder jumps that Ringo Chou couldn't do in the late '80s because his much-younger ACLs were starting to give. The hip was another matter; his pelvis felt torqued, the nerve canal raw all the way to his heel.

On the sixth step he took an oxy—that made two in an hour—then kept climbing. Sweating. He used to run the steps of mountain temples; how could these rickety beach house steps feel insurmountable? Oh, to be young again and riding those bedsprings like naughty Troy down there, having a time with the dark beauty who walked in on him in the bathroom. That was another thing: He'd been on that seat for forty-five minutes and hadn't moved his bowels because his organs felt jammed up. He'd felt like maybe he was getting somewhere when the pretty girl had entered and screamed.

Onward, he climbed. Up to his Malibu room with a view of the sea. The bed caught him cleanly, took the pain off his joints. A quarter moon hung over the gentle surge of water. He wished he could just relax and enjoy the first-class shelter from the storm this kid Troy was offering him. But it all felt so perishable, and too little too late.

The moon made him remember a girl . . .

. . .

It was 1993 and he was standing on the set of *City on Flame*, a giant tungsten moon hanging a fake glow over Victoria Harbor. He was already notorious among stuntmen, had already outlived the Shaw Brothers' '70s and the buddy-cop '80s. He had earned the scars and a reputation as high-flying Louie Mo, the guy you brought in when some arrogant A-lister wet his drawers two hundred feet up on a skyscraper, deciding that doing his own stunts wasn't such a good idea after all.

Louie stood on the docks, restless energy jittering in his legs, taking a hit off a cigarette, cracking a joke with the crew. Depression, like his two ex-wives, had been dogging him a little. Wine sometimes made it darker. His forbidden affair with Rebecca Lo, the Cantonese pop singer, sitting inside her movie star trailer at this very moment, made it deeper. But pulling off a big stunt—especially one where the movie star chickened out—filled some kind of dark hole inside, made him feel valued. There was no feeling like running seconds out ahead of explosions, knowing how many things could go wrong with pyrotechnics. If he tripped and Sammy the Fire Man sparked it off at the wrong time, he'd be torched in a ball of flame and shrapnel. That was one of the triggers to unleashing the Creature in his bloodstream: knowing how many things could go wrong.

On that night, lingering by the sheltered waters of the harbor—every now and then glancing toward the lights in Miss Lo's trailer—he was getting himself mentally prepped for the "Burning Boat" scene. As he paced and smoked, a set PA brought him a bulky cell phone. Call for Louie Mo.

Louie took the call, hoping it wasn't a lawyer tracking alimony. And then wishing it had been.

"Leave the set, my friend," Uncle Seven said in Cantonese. "These assholes are not playing fair, we're shutting down the movie. Whoever doesn't walk off the set tonight has made me lose face."

Uncle Seven, then a "Red Pole" member of the Heaven and Earth Society, never even gave Louie a chance to speak, just hung up. Louie saw all the eyes on him, could sense the tension over in the video village. He saw Jimmy Tang, the high-paid action star, getting his leather jacket on and heading toward his town car. He realized then that Jimmy Tang wasn't quite worming out of a dangerous stunt; he, too, had taken a call from Uncle Seven and wasn't going to cross him. He was leaving the set like a good boy.

Louie sidled up near Clifford Kwan, the director, got the story. They were already over budget, had no money to pay the Heaven and Earth Society—better known on the street as the 14K Triads—who were demanding a tax for filming on the harbor.

"Go home, Louie," Kwan said.

The irony of the dilemma wasn't lost on Louie. "We make movies about gangsters *with* gangsters," he once told Clifford. "*For* gangsters."

"Yeah," Clifford commiserated back then, "but it's been going on for four hundred years, man."

Clifford was right; the underworld operation known as the Triads had its roots in the late 1600s, when five Shaolin monk renegades teamed with Ming Dynasty loyalists to form the White Lotus Society. Their patriotic intentions back then were to overthrow the Qing Dynasty, but as the secret society of boxers evolved, they began to be viewed as a legitimate way of aiding immigrants from China as they tried to settle in new lands. Over time they became extortionists and launderers and traffickers, "like any other mafia," Clifford said. The booming Hong Kong movie industry of the '80s and '90s attracted them like wolves to goat herds.

At first, it was simple: You paid "lucky money" to get location permits or to protect crews filming in certain areas. If a production didn't pay, equipment was tampered with, film reels stolen, actors intimidated. Police protection was impossible to secure; the society ran too deep. By the late '80s the Triads became so embedded in the industry that some Dragon Heads like Uncle Seven began to catch the moviemaking bug, and started to produce their own films. If a star like Jimmy Tang didn't sign on to star in some low-budget gangster flick—movies about gangsters *made* by gangsters—he'd rue the day he said no. The same with Louie Mo and the Hong Kong stunt riggers. If Uncle Seven was producing a new movie, no matter how dreadful, that's what a stunt crew committed to, even if it meant passing on a high-end production that paid more. And the stunts were unregulated, highly dangerous. Resist the extortion and a man-on-fire death scene could become real, insurance paid out to the producers.

Now the extortion was spreading beyond the sets and the crews. Louie reminded Clifford of a recent incident just a few blocks away. Four reporters for *Affairs* magazine, a Hong Kong glossy, were attacked in their offices, brutally beaten, and hospitalized. Turned out that the magazine had published a critical review of a certain film and the starring actress. The Triads were running the business at every level. Not only did actors and crew have to commit to a Triad-produced movie, critics had to like it. In Hollywood, certain critics might be barred from future screenings if they turned up their noses at a film; in Hong Kong they got their noses broken or earlobes cut, offices ransacked. It was getting ugly.

"Are *you*?" Louie finally said. "Are *you* going home?"

Kwan didn't answer for a time. He looked gaunt and weary, like he had aged ten years over seven weeks of shooting. "We're one stunt away from having the movie in the can."

"Then we do it," Louie said. "I can do it in one take. Fast. Then we go home."

Kwan went silent again, just stood there, looking out at the lit-up harbor, his Hong Kong crew scurrying about. He nodded, barely.

While the shot was being set up, Louie went over to Rebecca Lo's trailer and knocked lightly. When she answered the door in her robe, he felt his heart quicken a tick. Barely thirty, she was the most beautiful woman in Hong Kong—and that wasn't just his estimation; it said so on the cover of several Asian pop culture magazines. There was also a rumor circulating that her face had been insured against injury or sun damage. That's how beautiful she was. On this night, however, she wore no makeup and appeared fearful, looking past Louie to see if anyone else was lingering in the shadows of honey wagons and portable toilets.

When she let him in, she double-locked the door, turned to him, and said, "You want your white alcohol? Or tea?"

Louie grabbed her and kissed her. She began to resist until she felt his strong arms pull her close, wrap around her. Protect her. He had always been something of her protector and they laughed often about how the world saw her as a "Deadly Beauty of Kung Fu," when what she really knew was ballet. It was Louie Mo who worked with her, showed her how to turn simple wushu stances or Shaolin animal poses into lethal and threatening expressions. It was all about the eyes, he told her. "Power from the eyes," he liked to say as he gently coached her lithe and petite frame into position. Her dancer's lines made it come easy; she was so flexible, she could nail a full split like a gymnast. In three days he had her throwing spinning back kicks that looked devastating, even if they contained none of the authentic internal power of the real *gongfu*.

"My *gongfu* is ugly," she would say, giggling with embarrassment and hiding her mouth behind her little doll-like hand.

"Yes," Louie would agree. "Very ugly. But your dancing? Beautiful."

It was after one of those early coaching sessions that they first kissed. Somewhere, in the back of his mind, Louie remembered it as the kiss that finalized his separation from Wife #2, even if his romance with the pop singer/movie star was a one-way street. She liked the thrill of an affair with a

tough guy stuntman, but that was the extent of it. If she was going to marry—he knew and she knew—it would be to a producer or a high-paid director like Kwan. Louie was just a bit of rough trade.

Yet, here they were on her sofa in the star wagon, shades down, place lit softly by a night-light. Her robe came away easily and her skin was warm and moisturized, smelling like jasmine and honey butter. Her breasts were perfect and tiny, nipples erect. So was he. She undid his buckle, released him from his jeans. They kissed insanely, made easy love. But Louie held back, refused to climax.

"Can't give away the *jing*," he would explain. His master had taught this to him years ago during his training. Before a fight, before a competition, and especially during the winter months, a man's essence must be conserved. Intercourse was permitted, and orgasm for the woman was encouraged; this only strengthened the man's *jing*. The restraint made Louie edgy, but it bolstered his *jing*. Four thousand years of Chinese science couldn't be wrong.

She tried, but couldn't talk him into a big finish. She had succeeded once, but when he went out to do a crash-through-glass-panel stunt, he was wobbly at the knees and felt strangely complacent, almost as if he had already done the stunt. He had smashed into a wood-and-sugar glass panel and merely splintered it. Being a perfectionist, this upset his world for a time and he swore to never surrender his *jing* within forty-eight hours of doing a stunt—never again—especially in the winter.

"Don't hold back," she whispered in his ear now. Louie

87

rolled off, forced himself back into his jeans, took a sip of the green tea that was steeping on a dresser, and fixed his hair in her mirror. When he looked at her she was in a sultry pose that made him rub his face furiously, almost comically. At the door he lightly banged his head several times to demonstrate his frustration. Yet, there was some kind of pride there, some strange joy in suffering.

"You aren't doing stunts tonight," she said. "Come back to me."

"I am doing stunt," he said.

"They will break your legs if you do. Don't be crazy."

"Already crazy."

He was tired of this game, he told her. Tired of getting himself mentally prepped for a stunt, only to have the set shut down by these lazy-ass bullies. Maybe he hit a turning point, or that chemical in the brain that produced fear had finally run dry, but the timid look in the eyes of the crew, and Rebecca Lo, sickened him. The first AD told Louie not to worry, there was going to be a protest march, denouncing the Triads. It would wend through the streets of Hong Kong, a parade led by several big Chinese movie stars. Jackie Chan was rumored to participate.

Parade, thought Louie Mo. *These criminals extort money from your movie and you respond with a parade? Why not a puppet show? Screw that.*

Back outside, on the set, he approached director Kwan with swagger in his catlike step. He flung his cigarette butt to the street, heeled it dead. "Let's go."

Thinking about that night now, all these years later,

Louie wished he had remained in Rebecca Lo's trailer and surrendered his *jing*. Drank some white alcohol, laid back on the sofa, telling her stories about his early days.

Of all the dangerous gags in his long, almost storied career, that one on the harbor, the "Burning Boat," would prove the most costly.

. . .

Zoe lay on her side, the curve of her big Eurasian hip buttered in moon glow. She studied Troy as he lay there, eyes on the ceiling, hair a sweat-drenched mess of ringlets. Not that they'd had sex. He had tried to touch her, but she wouldn't permit it; she wasn't that kind of girl, she told Troy, even as she lay naked beside him. She just wanted him to weigh the possibilities in the event he decided to invest more in her character.

"My father really likes you," she said. "He really thinks you're the next Tarantino."

"Your father's a passionate guy," Troy said, keeping his eyes off her. "I like how he puts his heart into projects that some people would just phone in, just for the money."

"You'd never do that, right? Too much of an artist. An auteur."

Troy got quiet, couldn't look at her. "I find my entry code on everything I do."

"What is it on *Slash*?"

"Zombie movies have a pedigree going back to German expressionist horror."

"Bullshit."

89

"What?"

"You hate this movie. I know you do. I saw it from day one; you looked like you'd rather be shooting *Real House-wives of Topanga Canyon*."

"Listen, I think with a nonlinear structure—"

"Come on, Troy. It wasn't your idea. You didn't write it."

She sat up now, reached for her dress. "It was my father's idea and it was a Go movie; you were impulsive."

"Maybe."

"Now you're stuck. And you only have three weeks."

"So you have to get naked and lie on my bed to have this conversation?"

"This is my house. I can get naked and lie on any bed and have any conversation I want."

"Like the time you came off the beach and did yoga in front of the TV while we were trying to watch the Super Bowl?"

"I just think there's some business shit you should know about. My father can't say it, he's got too much pride."

Troy could tell by her lifted ankles that she was now doing ab exercises, with a kind of subtle compulsion, right there beside him. "My dad didn't do so well with *Low Tide*. That was three straight-to-DVD flicks in a year. After that, no one would touch him. Couldn't get arrested."

"He's got a lot riding on this one, I know."

"More than that, Troy. He couldn't get any investors behind this one."

"He used his own money?"

"Worse."

"What's worse than using your own money?"

"Using Ortega Garza's money."

"Who the fuck is Ortega Garza?"

"He's from Guatemala."

"The foreign investor, okay, right."

"Then there's the white hip-hop guys from Alhambra. Invested company money if my father uses their soundtrack."

"I hate that soundtrack."

"Me too. And these two Albanian brothers from the east coast always wanted to see their name in the credits."

"So you're saying—"

"I'm saying that if you don't turn in a movie on a shoe-string that looks like twenty million, my father could get hurt. Big-time."

"And why don't you think I'll come through?"

He looked at her as she wriggled back into her impossibly small mocha number and fished for the zipper.

"Because I saw your film from Austin. I saw the passion. You're better than this shit, and there's the chance you just might say, 'Damn the torpedoes, I'm going for broke.'"

Troy propped himself up on pillows, watching Zoe zip her dress hard. For a chick who Durbin deemed vapid, Avi's daughter had uncanny intuition. She seemed to know that Troy wasn't sitting up late at night working on *Slash*. So it all seemed merely a head game when she asked the question, "When do we shoot my new scene?"

"I need to polish it."

"Then get back to it, Troy Boy. Nine-millimeter. I blow her ginger tits off."

"So *that's* how you kill a zombie," Troy said.

She slipped out quietly, as if not to disturb the Asian houseguest, then she edged back in with a closing thought. "Maybe you just found your entry code."

Troy looked out at the moon over the choppy surf and let a breath escape in taut increments. There was that asthma thing again, as thick as the perfume scent in his sheets. It was like she'd marked the property, like she wanted any girl he slept with to know she held rank and first right of refusal.

"Did you just threaten me?" He was chasing her now, but the house was empty and her keys were gone from the counter.

11

HAPPY HOUR

"Patrón silver, on the rocks, squeeze of lime," Banazak said, sitting at the empty bar at the Marina del Rey Hotel. Then he realized, as his eyes adjusted to the dark, that it wasn't entirely empty. A woman sat at the far end. A Marina divorcée from the '80s, he figured; a holdout, still single, same big hair, but now sun-leathered, gin-numb, and staring at the TV. She glanced hungrily at his muscles on occasion, but he kept his eyes on the bar mirror so he could see who might come in.

Carlos, the barman, had just set down his tequila when he caught sight of Papagallo's reflection. In his bright Hawaiian shirt and hustler's walk, you couldn't miss the guy. He waved, took a seat at the far corner table, and pulled a wafer-thin laptop from his bag. "Sit over here near me, big guy," Papagallo said, turning the computer on. He ordered the same drink as Banazak before even figuring out what it was. Banazak moved a chair like it was made of paper, turned it backward, and sat with his big arms hanging over the backrest. "What you find?"

"You already saw the security tape from Palm Springs, the Chinese guy in the hotel. Had the football."

"Yeah, yeah."

"I got the tape from outside, in the parking lot. Here you go."

Papagallo ran the clip: the little Chinese guy with framed jersey and football, hurrying the stuff into the backseat of a Chevy, shutting the door, looking all around. He got into the passenger seat and the Chevy skid out. "There's the plate, see?"

"You track it?"

"Yeah. Registered to an old car that was sold to a junk-yard in the valley, then crushed. It's a dead plate, dummy plate."

Banazak drummed his fingers on the chair rest, staring at the frozen image of the car. "How do we find them?"

"I know you don't want a shit storm, you know, all that other stuff to come up with these chicks looking for money. I can put the word out on the street. LAPD will put it on their watch. If we spot the car, I'll call you."

Banazak downed the silver tequila, crushed some ice and lime in his molars. "When I kill this chink, wouldn't it be ironic if his body goes in a trunk to the same junkyard where he got the dummy plate?"

"You don't want to do that, Jay," Papagallo said, almost fatherly.

"Yes, I do," Banazak said.

Papagallo looked into the big man's eyes and saw that he meant it. Something wasn't right, somewhere in the former Raider's head. Too many concussions, too many growth hormones, too many nights of snorting blow on the boat on Bali Way. It was like he almost forgot about the football; he couldn't even sleep anymore, from that need to kill the Chinese thief he'd slugged it out with on the rooftops of Monterey Park. He felt eyes in the back of his neck; he snapped his head around. The big-haired woman was staring at him, her eyes at half-mast.

"Cougar," Banazak said to the detective.

"Yeah, right," Papagallo said, finishing his tequila. "From the La Brea Tar Pits."

12

THE CAGE

INT. NUMBER 9 BAR—NIGHT

CHO looks up at the clock, it reads: 9:10.
BUZZ sets a plate of hot food before him. Cho
can't seem to identify it.

> BUZZ
> For you, my friend, a Chinese
> twist on the French classic coq
> au vin. The Number 9 is known for
> its Asian fusion. Best in L.A.

Cho nods in appreciation. Buzz watches him
taste it.

> BUZZ (CONT'D)
> Fucking Uncle Johnny, man . . .

As Cho chews, he tries to read Buzz's point.

                    BUZZ (MORE)
          He always talked out both sides
          of his ass. He finally burn you
          one too many times, or what?

                    CHO
          I'm done. That's all. Can't fight
          above ground, and I don't want to
          work their game anymore.

                    BUZZ
98   No money?

                    CHO
          They make money. But they won't
          make any more off me.

                    BUZZ
          What kind of stakes does Uncle
          Johnny raise these days? What
          kind of purse?

Cho gets quiet, searches for the best way to
couch it.

                    CHO
          How much is a human life worth?

DOG BEACH

CHO (CONT'D)
These fights only end one way. Some
people pay big bucks to see it.

Buzz is either disturbed or intrigued or both
when—

MONEY (O.S.)
Yo, I want to buy a beer for that
man . . .

MONEY, a Thai kid, is anchored down the bar,
paying for his beer with a sweaty fold of cash.

MONEY (CONT'D)
'Cause I think I know who he is.

CHO
You know this guy?

Buzz nods, smirks.

BUZZ
I'll get rid of him.

CHO
Don't start a scene.

Buzz moves down to the loud Thai kid.

BUZZ

What's up, Money?

MONEY

I want to buy a beer for Mr.
Lightning Fist down there.

BUZZ

This is a night where I don't
want any trouble in my place.
Come back tomorrow.

100 Money ignores the owner and backs away from the
bar to create some space. He stares at Cho's
back; Cho watches him calmly in the bar mirror.

MONEY

You talk for yourself, Lightning
Fist? Or you let a *Gwailo* do your
talking? I said I want to buy you
a beer.

CHO

Thanks, man. I had my drink. You
go sit down and have one.

MONEY

You telling me to sit down? What
are you, my school teacher?

> CHO
>
> If I was your school teacher, I'd
> take a ruler to your ass, punk.

Money's eyes go infernal.

> CHO
>
> Go sit down.

Money unzips his jacket, shifts his weight
onto his back foot. The CROWD senses trouble,
goes quiet.

> MONEY
>
> Turn around, champ.

Weary-eyed, Cho turns around and eyes the kid.

> MONEY (CONT'D)
>
> There's a smoker across the
> river. Either we go there and do
> it, or we do it right here.

> CHO
>
> Do what?

> MONEY
>
> Funny man, huh? You ever hear the
> name Money? Thirty-one fights,

MONEY (MORE)

all knockouts. I want you to be
number thirty-two.

CHO

I don't want to be number thirty-
two. I want to sit here and
listen to the music and eat
this Chinese twist on a French
classic. So go sit down and stop
making trouble.

(MARGIN NOTE: Too much English dialogue for
Louie. Just say "Go sit down.")

102

Money nods. Not in acceptance, but as if to
say, "Okay, this can only end one way, so here
we go." He turns around to scout the corners
and calculate distance . . . he casts off his
jacket.

And then he WHEELS INTO AN ATTACK that is so
fast it has to impress Cho.

Cho meets the attack with a 180-degree SPIN-
NING KICK that sends Money CRASHING through
tables and breaking a mirror. WOMEN SCREAM,
people begin to clear . . .

• • •

Cheers filled Dog House as Troy ran the scene on his big monitor. Malone, T-Rich, Durbin, and Louie were all grouped behind him, drinking Coronas. "Now, just wait," Troy said.

They did.

Then the music started. Hard, driving metal triggered a flurry of images across the screen: Louie Mo rolling across the hood of the Chevy, landing and firing a barrage of chain punches, then rolling back onto the hood and executing a backflip.

The Dogs cheered in unison as the reel sped up: jerky kicks, staccato punches, wushu hands, and Wing Chun blocks, all building to a frenzied tempo of clips from some of the greatest vintage Hong Kong fight footage of all time. A narrator crooned low, as if channeling his inner James Earl Jones—it was T-Rich, who was good with voices: "For three decades, behind every legendary Hong Kong fight hid a man with no name. A man who made it all possible, even when it was *impossible*. . . . NOW, for the first time . . . he steps out from behind the stars to shine on his own. The man Bey Logan calls the greatest stuntman in the history of Hong Kong cinema—Louie Mo. Out from the shadows and into . . . *The Cage*."

"Louie Mo," they all hollered and hooted, and Louie, Corona in hand, shrugged. Shrugged but couldn't hide a smile.

"Who is seeing this commercial?" Louie said.

103

"Who is seeing this *what?*"

"Who is seeing this?"

"The fucking world, Louie," Troy said. He raised his bottle in a toast. "This is called the sizzle reel. The buzz."

As the Dogs continued to celebrate, Louie excused himself, went out onto the back porch, just him and the slow roar of the night surf.

"He all right?" T-Rich said.

"Yeah," said Troy, rewinding the teaser. "He gets a little emotional. He's finally getting his own movie, man. Malone?"

Malone was just staring, pondering the sizzle reel with an oddly detached look on his face.

"What do you think?"

Malone scratched the ginger scruff on his chin, his eyes glassy slits. "YouTube," he drawled. "Cut this puppy viral, bro. This is a game changer."

104

known on the set of a Peter Hu movie, he missed the Google. Missed "the Facebook," too. Those Internet tools were banned in China, but here in Hong Kong they were wide-open portals. Back when Tiger Eye was riding a sport bike in the streets as part of the Heaven and Earth Society's 49, it wasn't so easy to track accounts. Cabaret acts, television shows, and movie productions could be slippery, moving in and out before the Triads even knew they were working. But the Google was like free surveillance if you knew how to use it. Just type in "movies filming in Hong Kong" or the name of a sneaky producer and the screen lit up with articles, videos, and links-within-links that could take you inside the offices of the Hong Kong Film Fund. That's what Tiger Eye liked about the entertainment business; it was made up of natural braggers and self-promoters. Easy to track.

"How about Koi Lam?" Tiger Eye said in Cantonese.

"Paid," said Johnny Yee, making a check mark on his iPad.

"King Jiang?"

"King Jiang is not paid."

Tiger Eye grew quiet for a moment. "Give him until end of week. Then send the Little Brothers." He clicked back to the next page on his computer, scanned, and was ready to close out when something caught his one good eye. He stared at the link for a long moment, the one that read: Legendary Stuntman Hong Kong Louie Mo New Movie YouTube.

"We finish?" said Johnny Yee, but Tiger Eye did not respond. His good eye widened slightly and he tapped on the

13

HONG KONG

The Swiss handgun, a SIG Sauer Mosquito, rested on the table just an easy reach from the wireless mouse. Cao sat over the keypad in a large open-floor office, focusing intently. With a glass eye and his longish black hair chopped in layers, he resembled an exotic bird on a perch. "Chen Jinbao," he said, scrolling down names and reading them off to another man, a stout guy named Johnny Yee, who made notes on an iPad. Both men wore suits, as did the five or six who were busying themselves at long card tables laid out with watches, handbags, blue jeans, Northface parkas, and endless racks of bootleg DVDs.

The guys at the tables seemed to be taking inventory of product, but not Tiger Eye Cao. His eye replacement wasn't actually glass, it was tiger eye gemstone, polished to an amber shine; it gave him the chilling stare of a big cat, even now as he focused on "the Google," as he called it. Having been over on the mainland for the past two weeks, making his presence blue link, brought up YouTube. When Johnny Yee heard the name, he left his folding chair with such force he nearly tipped it. Leaning over Tiger Eye's computer, he watched the teaser unfold with urgent fight choreography, set to a heavy metal soundtrack: "LOUIE MO," the narrator said. "Out from the shadows and into . . . *The Cage*." The screen faded to black and COMING SOON bled through in dramatic red font.

"Mother*shit*," Cao said in English. Then he hit play again. . . .

• • •

Uncle Seven sat in the lounge of the Peninsula Hotel in a big, overstuffed leather chair, modestly picking his teeth from behind a napkin. He had arrived in one of the Rolls-Royce Phantom limousines in the hotel fleet, punctual as always. It was Thursday and happy hour at the Peninsula featured the Carpenters singing their greatest hits. The girl had the same long hair as Karen Carpenter and sang just like her except for the accent on certain words. The Chinese Richard double just sat and played piano, daintily sipping ginger ale in between songs.

Uncle Seven never missed the act; those '70s songs were like a tribute to his own greatest era. In his herringbone suit and muted tie, he'd sit at his special table to the right of the stage, nosing and sipping the most expensive single malt whiskey in the hotel. Around him sat sub-bosses and van-guards, those long-suffering underlings he forced to come hear the Carpenters' clone act. Standing off a ways was a special bodyguard with an earbud like a Secret Service agent. The hotel itself positioned a security man, also with an earbud, not far away.

During the music set, Uncle Seven stared with a knotted, somber expression, bottom lip pressed outward. Any tourist might have thought he was just some scowling old businessman picking his teeth. But when the piano started "We've Only Just Begun," he surrendered a slight smile and emotion showed in his eyes. Sometimes, toward the end of that particular number, when the girl would switch to Cantonese, Uncle Seven would feel his eyes pool up and he'd remove his tortoiseshell glasses, stanch a tear. The Chinese Karen Carpenter would smile sweetly at him. One night he had six dozen white roses delivered to the stage only minutes after giving the orders.

Now he noticed that the hotel's security man, muscular in a white dress shirt and black vest, was questioning someone trying to get into the lounge. Two of Uncle Seven's men went over, straightened it out, and led Tiger Eye Cao inside. At the table, the Triad with the glass eye and birdlike feathery hair bowed to the elder. Uncle Seven nodded, gestured for him to sit, gestured for someone to pour the man a dram of the imported scotch. Tiger Eye did, after all, hold the rank of White Paper Fan, a position high up in the Triads organization.

When the song ended to a smattering of applause, Tiger Eye leaned near the old man, whispered in his ear. The aging godfather couldn't hear well over the applause, so he shifted his body and Tiger Eye half-stood to deliver a second try.

DOG BEACH

When Uncle Seven heard the name, a dark look passed over him. For a moment, it appeared that he was choking on salty bar nuts. He coughed hard into his napkin, kept coughing. The men at the table and hotel security, and even the Chinese Karen Carpenter, were all looking anxiously toward him. When the cough subsided and he swallowed some scotch, the piano player started playing "Yesterday Once More." Uncle Seven sat back and smiled. His men knew he wasn't smiling at the girl; he was smiling at the news that Tiger Eye Cao had just delivered. It teased an almost youthful smile from his ancient face. Revenge was a dish best served with a dram of sixteen-year-old Lagavulin and a drop of water to open it up. Number 8 of the 36 Oaths: Make a sworn brother lose face, you shall be killed by myriad swords.

14

CHINESE MONEY

Morning broke with a tide so high it lapped at the rotting stilts of Dog House and brought in a swirl of sea trash and hungry gulls. Troy was humpbacked at his Mac, in his boxers, reading down through the comments on his YouTube teaser. He was trying not to get too big a head from a litany of AWESOME, or too depressed from WTF?? and THIS WILL SUCK. Someone actually knew his name from the Austin Film Fest and wrote a thoughtful blurb on his earlier heist film, calling him unpretentious and a breath of fresh air. He wondered if it was his Aunt Rose in New Jersey.

Then he read an odd-looking comment that had some Chinese characters attached beneath: *Very good taste movie. Our company is very much hopeful to consider foreign distribution. We release movie in rather big foreign market. See our link and contact. Hello!*

The name at the bottom, near the Chinese characters read "CINE WORLD FILM MARKETING, HONG KONG." Troy felt a slight rush, hit the link. The site was simple and unadorned, with the choice of Chinese, English, or Deutsch. Spare but professional, it listed several produced titles that Troy knew. Cine World, the site advertised, also owned a chain of movie theaters across China.

With Dutch having a morning smoke and coffee on the back porch, and Louie and the Dogs asleep in their respective chambers, Troy sent an e-mail to the link, expressing his interest. By six that night he had gone back and forth twice with a Mr. Xia.

It was with great pleasure, Mr. Xia wrote, and with "fortuitous timing" that Cine World would be sending some buyers to New York and Los Angeles. He said he would love to meet the director and discuss.

"It just goes to prove, man," Troy told Durbin, who had come home with a restock of beers. "You follow your passion, things fall into place. It gets contagious, brother."

"Give me some of that contagion, man. New Line passed on my spec. They said it felt familiar."

"Never say die, Durbin."

"What about *Slash*? You got what—two weeks?"

"Here's the plan," Troy said, taking a semi-cold beer from Durbin's grocery bag. "In two, three weeks, when Avi's just about ready to come cut my head off, I send a DVD over to Lantana. No cover letter, no note. Just let him watch and get blown away. Then I drop the bomb, tell him what I did, and tell him that he owns *The Cage*. He owns a piece of movie history, he owns a hit. Then, if everything goes right with this Chinese company, I hit him with the closer and tell him we've also got foreign distribution across all of Asia."

"Jesus, bro."

"Forget *Slash*, he'll be paying back his investors with a return they never dreamed of. It's a win-win, love-fest, you're-a-fucking-genius-Troy situation."

"It sounds risky."

"Ask Louie Mo about risk," Troy said. "Ask Louie Mo what it feels like to ride on top of the Shanghai bullet train with no wires."

He had Durbin's attention, so he drove one last point home: "Forget trying to win the spec lottery with another gratuitous frat comedy. Write from the heart, bro. Write what you know."

Durbin stared at him for a long moment. "My life *is* a gratuitous frat comedy. It *is* what I know. And I'm passionate about it."

Troy ruminated, but didn't know what to say.

A toasted voice came from a chair where Malone sat, waiting on a whale sighting. "Go with God, bro. We're all just one failure away from selling star maps and hand jobs in front of the Motherlode."

"Thank you, Deepak," Durbin said. Then Troy's cell phone came alive with the *Enter the Dragon* theme: Old school jazz, funky wah-wah pedal, and jungle scream. It was a ringtone that Troy had set for Louie Mo and everyone loved it.

"Yeah, Louie, hey."

Troy listened to Louie, cast his eyes up toward the stairs. "Come on down and get a fish taco, man."

Louie called from upstairs often; it was his office, he said. Descending the stairs was a chore best made only once a day. Now, as he made his careful descent, dressed in his red sweat suit, he stopped to look around. He never knew who he'd find at Dog House on any given day: Dutch in the living room, talking famous car chases with Durbin; T-Rich asleep on the floor with *L.A. Weekly*. Or Malone and Troy, unwrapping fish tacos and jabbering like excited schoolboys about *Sukiyaki Western Django*. Louie joined them at the kitchen table, unwrapping a fish taco like he was too tired, or too queasy, to eat. "What scene tomorrow?" he wanted to know.

"I left your call sheet under your door. You fight the Brazilian twins on the beach, up at Point Dume."

"Jumping off rocks?"

"Yeah. Like we rehearsed."

Louie winced at the thought. "Should have filmed rehearse."

"Should we get you a stunt double?"

Louie threw the fish taco wrapper at Troy. The director fended it off, laughing. "How about I kill you?" Louie said. "First the Brazil twins, then you. For making me do this."

Troy laughed harder, watching Louie double-clutch the messy taco and take a tired bite.

• • •

The fly-off-the-rocks stunt at the Point went off like gangbusters. No matter how he griped, when the camera rolled, Louie Mo harnessed the adrenaline and pushed himself through scar tissue and stiff hips. The Brazilian twins were charismatic team players, and Louie choreographed a clever way to dispatch them both with a reverse crescent kick he called "two-cut eyebrow."

The boys applauded him after every take. Then, after the final shot of the day, the one Troy always called "the martini," they bumped knuckles, slapped his back, and took him and Dutch for sushi and beer at Zuma Beach. Malone suggested they stop calling the final shot of each day the martini, and begin calling it the brewski because that's all they drank. No, said Louie. He loved the sound of Troy calling out the martini and Troy was the director. The boss.

Over sushi, Louie told stories about some of his most dangerous stunts. The guys laughed at the way Troy would fill in the blanks when Louie couldn't remember the name of an actor or the order of an action sequence. "On that crazy movie," Louie would say, "I smash through the glass and the director . . ."

Without missing a beat, Troy would quietly fill the gap, say, "Tsui Hark," not even looking up from his spicy tuna roll. Louie would stare, bewildered, then surrender a knuckle bump.

The boys would howl over another round of beers.

"With all his concussions," Dutch said to Troy, "he needs you with him to finish his memories."

"Almost burned head off," Louie said, trying to top his own accounts. "John Woo movie. I am double for Chow Yun Fat."

"A *Better Tomorrow II*," Troy said. "When the house fucking blows and Chow's head catches on fire."

115

"Me," Louie said, then sipped his beer.

Troy was lost in thought now, making connections to sequences in his mind. *"City on Flame,"* he said. "Directed by Clifford Kwan. That chick, man."

Louie seemed disinterested now, more focused on his beer than another story.

"Rebecca Lo," Troy kept going. "She was hot."

"Yeah" was all Louie said, and now he seemed to be looking for the waiter, like he wanted to pay the bill and go.

"Whatever happened to her? Rebecca Lo."

"I can't remember."

"Too many falls on his head," Dutch said.

"I fucking *love* that scene in *Dragon Cop* when she fights the fat dude on the bar."

"Stupid movie, I don't remember," Louie said, growing restless now as Troy played to Malone and Durbin.

"She's a stripper," he explained, "and she pole dances while beating the shit out of, like, ten motherfuckers."

"Okay," Louie said, forcing a smile, "no more talking about stupid Hong Kong movie." But Troy was worked up, even trying to YouTube the sequence on his phone.

"She's spinning on the pole and throwing kicks, and then she spins down to one knee and there's a close-up, just her eyes. She says, 'Me love you long time,' then pulls a fucking metal hair pin and throws it—"

Louie lashed out suddenly. Violently. He knocked over Troy's Corona. And Durbin's, too. "I said, stop talking about all this stupid kung fu movie!"

The table went still. Malone slid his chair back, mopped some spilled beer from his baggies.

"Whoa," Dutch said, calming the stuntman.

"Easy, bro," Troy said. He was looking cautiously into the eyes of the washed-up stunt player, thought he saw something dark there. Something unpredictable. Something he hadn't seen before, except a hint back when Louie had punched the Thai kickboxer in the face.

"I'm sorry," Louie said, righting the tipped beer bottle and using napkins to sop the spill. "Headache."

"He gets headaches," Dutch said.

"No worries," Troy said, but he felt that same sense of distrust he did when Dutch first walked through the Dog House. What kind of loose cannons were these folks? Were they on bath salts or some shit?

T-Rich took the curse off. "Troy can get carried away. Don't ever get him started on the final gun fight in *El Mariachi*."

"Let's go home," Louie said. His fifth Corona was dry.

HONG KONG, 1993—NIGHT

Louie shimmied up the mast of the sailboat as it went up in a vertical flame the color of hot teal. Fire licked at his ostrich-skin loafers as he squirreled to the boom then clung there, waiting for the breakaway. The radio crackled and Sammy the Fire Man yelled in Cantonese from an unseen perch. The mast began to topple, flames and sparks sweeping

117

over the mainsail as he held tightly, riding the falling mast over the dark waters.

As the passing speedboat roared by, Louie timed it to perfection. His hands, gelled with thermal barrier, were burning, but he held on two seconds longer, then let go. He landed in the hull and deftly turned his loss of balance into a whirling ax kick, knocking the pilot overboard and seizing the wheel. The wind caught his Jimmy Tang wig just right. No one would ever know it was not Jimmy Tang.

Maybe it was his determination to work in the face of Uncle Seven's threats, but Louie pulled it off in one take. The applause was spare — most of the crew had gone home — but he felt the surge inside overtaking the stubborn depression; the Creature in his bloodstream made him feel alive and ready for a drink.

"*Ho zang ah!*" yelled director Kwan, patting Louie's shoulder. "Very excellent!"

Louie navigated a gauntlet of hand slaps and congratulations and, apologizing for the thermal gel still on his hands, wended his way through the clutter of cables and trailers and camera trucks, moving down the little lane to Miss Lo's honey wagon. He'd take her up on that *Baijiu*, the white alcohol now. And, if she was game, maybe finish where he left off. Big finish. Or maybe spend an hour, sitting on the sofa, just being with her.

He knocked on the honey wagon door then remembered he was still wearing that stupid Jimmy Tang wig. He yanked it off, tucked it in his back pocket, and knocked again. Still no answer.

He looked around for an AD. He wanted to get a twenty on her, but it was getting late and the set was about dead.

He found the door unlocked, peered in. Called her name. Nothing. Maybe she left the set like the others, he surmised, afraid to defy the Triads. Such bullshit; so wrong.

When he called her apartment and only got her answering machine, he took a cab over to Prince Edward Terrace and buzzed her door. Again, no answer. But from inside, he could hear a sound like crying. Quiet whimpering from deep in the apartment.

He hit the buzzer again, then knocked, called her name. Finally, he rounded the corner and went up a fire escape to the second floor. He let himself in through a bedroom window, called her name cautiously. Following the whimpering sound, he moved on carefully, his quiet feet heading down the hall toward the top of the stairs.

She was kneeling on the carpet, her back to him, trembling all over. He called her name again, her Chinese name, and when she turned, he saw the horror. Her face, the most beautiful woman in Hong Kong, had been sliced in a crisscross of tracks, as if by a box cutter.

Louie couldn't move at first. Then he threw himself to his knees, got close to her. Her mouth had been cut at the edges into a clown-like grin, like a Chinese opera mask. Like broken porcelain. Louie yelled out in anguish. . . .

• • •

All of this coursed through Louie's memory in a matter of seconds; quick images, desaturated color. No sound except

119

for a deep pulse. Kind of the way John Woo would have shot it in his glory days. Then it was gone. He would think no more on it and he hoped the kid would never bring her name up again.

The next day, a touch of the headache lingered, but it was back to work. After recording some wild lines and wrapping for the afternoon, Dutch drove him over to North Hollywood to take care of some business. On the way, Louie was talking about the boys. How much he liked them even though he couldn't figure them out. So immature, he said. Laughing when they fart, playing video games, smoking weed.

"Thresholders," Dutch said, and when Louie looked over at her, she lit another cigarette and explained. "They're on the threshold of adulthood, but they're not ready to go through the door yet. The Dog House, man. It's like their haven."

Louie made no reply, but, she noted, as they rolled their way closer to the location, he kept glancing in the side mirror, or angling a look over his shoulder.

"What is it?" Dutch said.

"Just looking," he said. "So much traffic."

But when they pulled into a little strip mall, he kept watching a car that had been behind them. When it kept going, he relaxed. "This is a bad place."

"Yeah, I guess," she said.

"After I finish the movie, maybe I leave."

"And go where?"

"I don't know. Depends."

"On what?"

"How movie does." And then, he said, almost sheepishly, "Maybe sequel, I don't know."

Dutch burst out laughing. "Sequel? *Dude*. You're not going to be able to walk again after this movie."

Louie grew quiet with that thought. His hip was killing him, lending credence to her point.

"How about you?" he said finally.

"What about me?"

"Where will you go?"

Dutch grew quiet, blew out some cigarette smoke like it didn't matter, and she didn't care.

"You go back home," Louie said. "Marry cowboy."

Dutch looked at him over the rims of her nicked-up shades and managed a smile. "You marrying me off? Who's going to drive you everywhere?"

Louie was counting money now, sealing it in an envelope. "Be right back," he said.

When he limped down the sidewalk and entered the little law office, she shook her head and scoffed a laugh. "Sequel. Jesus."

Since the two took up together, over a year ago now, she'd been driving him to this sad, little strip mall whenever he scored some cash. He'd always do the same thing: count off some bills, put them in an envelope, seal it, and go inside for about twenty minutes. She stopped asking him about it because he never answered. She just figured it was to wire alimony to his two ex-wives, the bane of his existence that he sometimes called "the Two-Headed Dragon."

He had a daughter in Hong Kong, he told her once, but

one of the dragons had poisoned the child's mind against him. Called him a womanizer, a drinker, a reckless, crazy motherfucker. Dutch always laughed to herself when he'd throw his arms up at that accusation as if it hardly stood to reason. The guy must have been a handful in his younger days; shit, he was an *armful now*. But driving him in and out of gags gave her a reason to get out of bed in the morning. Maybe Louie did need her, like she said, but she needed him, too. Not that she'd ever tell him that.

When he got back in the car, he was handling a hot slice of pizza from the joint next to the law office. He gently handed it to her and settled into his seat. "Let's go. Back to Dog House."

• • •

The next few days of shooting went so well Troy was nearly giddy. The movie was snowballing, production feeding off the breakneck pace of the script itself. *Run, Lola, Run* was proving an apt reference. Durbin, looking at forty-five minutes of cut footage, joked that it should be called *House of Flying Red Bull*.

With less than twelve days till his *Slash* deadline, Troy got the e-mail he was waiting for. Representatives from the Chinese company were in Los Angeles and eager to meet. They had a full dance card, they said, with a lot of big meetings with American producers, but they would meet Troy at any time, even late at night if necessary. They also asked, quite shyly, if it was possible to meet Louie Mo. They would buy breakfast or dinner at a very nice place. Troy suggested tea at the Coffee Bean, the one on PCH, right up the road from Dog Beach.

When Troy told Louie and asked him to come, the stuntman grew edgy. "This is American movie," he said, pointing a disciplinary finger. "Why now you are bringing in Chinese money?"

"Louie, man, co-prod is how it gets done these days. This is huge."

"I don't go. I don't like these kind of people."

Troy could almost understand; stuntmen weren't the personality types who gave good sit-downs, or suffered suits gladly. Troy would do the honors, keep his star behind the scenes and on a pedestal.

So, at five minutes to nine on an overcast Friday, he threw on a leather jacket he hadn't worn since New York, put on his shades, and drove his tiny Mini-Cooper up the beach.

The four Chinese businessmen were already there, ritualistically punctual and sitting around an outdoor table with tall cups of tea. Troy approached the table, looking every bit the young American film rebel. Handshakes, smiles, and Troy's overwrought bow made the rounds.

The guy who seemed to be in charge, the one with a headful of choppy layers and tiny, expensive sunglasses, gestured for Troy to sit first. Ordering an iced mocha with a double shot, Troy tried not to look too nervous. Truth was, he loved these kinds of meetings. They brought out a surge of energy that, with four swallows of strong coffee, spiked his enthusiasm high. He would try not to talk too fast, but he did anyway, mentioning the names of the film titles associated with Cine World.

"You speak good Chinese," said the one with the feathered hair. The other three all smiled, laughed, and expressed a kind of amazement over Troy's command of Mandarin.

"Only movie titles," he said. "And certain kung fu moves."

"Kung fu," laughed the stout one in the red tie. He did a clichéd attempt at a martial arts pose and laughed some more. They all seemed genuinely appreciative and amused that Troy even knew the term "kung fu."

After conveying their interest in the YouTube teaser and the "good taste story" and the inspired concept of relaunching an old-school stuntman in the new era of action film, the one with the layered hairdo removed his shades. His right eye stopped Troy dead. It resembled a tiger eye marble, amber and striped through with black. It seemed to gaze wall-eyed at the traffic on PCH while the other eye, handsome black, glinted at the young American. "My boss very much desires to meet Louie Mo," he said in an educated British accent. "He is at American Film Market today, but perhaps later."

With two formal hands he presented a business card to Troy. "That's my card, the hotel name is on the reverse. Quite near the airport."

"LAX," said the stout one, whose English was not as good, let alone refined, but his laughter made him likable. When Troy tried to redirect the conversation back to the chain of movie theaters in China, and the potential for a distribution deal, the one with the glass marble eye kept finding a way to bring it back to his boss's keen desire to meet the star. "These things make him happy. He likes to meet the stars. It makes his—"

"Confidence," the stout one said. "Gives him the confidence, you know, for the investment."

"Got it," Troy said. "But my actor is in character and he just can't meet right now."

The looks around the table fell moody. Their boss must really take his star-fucking seriously, Troy mused.

"You will ask Mr. Louie Mo again?" Tiger Eye said.

"I'll try."

"My boss is in meetings all day. If you bring Louie to LAX hotel tonight, everything will be simpatico. We shall make the deal."

"You'll make the deal? Without seeing a cut?"

"My boss has already seen it," Tiger Eye said, lightly touching a finger to his temple. "In here. Good mind. Good mind for movies." This seemed to trigger laughter too, and Troy laughed along.

"I hear you," he said. "These days, it's not 'What's the story?' it's 'What's the poster?'"

The Chinese laughed even harder, but Troy didn't really think they got the joke. Finally, it was good-byes and handshakes and Troy bowing again. The stout one found Troy's bow quite respectful, so he patted the young man's shoulder. Then, like a playful uncle at a picnic, he broke into that mock kung fu stance again. Everyone laughed as they went to their cars.

Driving south past Moonshadows, Troy noticed that the

Chinese team's vehicle, a rented Lexus, had followed him out into the racetrack flow of PCH traffic. He felt oddly responsible for them, like they were his foreign guests, so he kept watching in the rearview to make sure they were okay.

When he pulled over to find a parking place at Dog Beach, they, too, slowed down, a dangerous maneuver on Highway 1. Horns blared, but the silver Lexus hovered and Troy could see three of the four, craning and looking toward where he had parked. Troy honked and waved. About one hundred yards north, one of the Chinese finally wriggled an arm out his window and waved good-bye, all smiles, like an overeager tourist.

Troy sat for a moment, drumming the wheel and feeling hopeful. He was going to have to drop the hammer on Louie Mo. The dude was going to have to suck it up and take a ride to the airport, sit around a bad Holiday Inn with the boss, and speak Chinese. The upside was huge.

126

• • •

Back at Dog House, Dutch came out of the bathroom, found Louie sitting in his favorite shabby-chic chair, and said, "Come on, man, don't tell me this."

"Tell you what?"

"You peeing blood?"

"Why?"

"Just answer me."

Louie grew sullen for a beat. "Bruising the kidney. From Lau Kar-Leung movie. Long time ago."

"Jesus," Dutch said. "You should go to the ER."

DOG BEACH

When Louie waved her off, she sniffed. "Stubborn bastard. You shouldn't be doing this."

"Last one."

"Yeah, last one. Don't let this kid kill you."

"What do we shoot tomorrow? Fight? Or big dialogue?"

"How do I know? I think this guy's making it up as he goes." As she started for the porch, Louie got up, tried not to grimace.

"Hey," he said, removing a fold of cash from his pocket. He peeled off several one-hundred-dollar bills.

Dutch looked at him, confused. He had already given her three grand in cash from his advance, said it was for her driving and for all the gas. "What's this?"

"Find the football."

"The what?"

"I can't sleep. Bad dreams, the man chasing me. Wants the football."

"That why you've been looking over your shoulder, like someone's on our ass?"

"Go find it. Bring to him, to the boathouse. Give it back to him."

"You're serious."

Louie looked her in the eye until she took the cash. Troy entered from the back porch, tossed his bomber jacket on the couch with a flair of triumph. "Met with China."

Louie studied him, waiting for more.

"They want to make a distribution deal, based on the teaser."

"I don't know about that kind of business."

127

"Louie. All you have to do is go with me and meet the boss—"

"I told you no," he said, pressing Troy like he did when he first jumped him in the house and ordered him to pay his boss. "You understand me? I don't meet these kind of fucking people."

"Then I won't get the fucking deal."

"Then you don't get fucking deal. Fuck you, Troy."

Dutch shook her head at the calamity, at the blood she had seen in the toilet, at the whole crazy arrangement. "I'm out of here," she said, and she was.

"Louie, listen—"

"No, *you* listen to me. I have two divorce in Hong Kong. Too many wife, they chase me. Lawyers, too. They look everywhere for me. Why you put the trailer on the YouTube?"

"Louie, this movie is going global. Viral. Your name is going to be out there, you have to deal, dude. This is your time in the sun."

"I don't go meet the Chinese business."

"Okay. Forget it, man. I'll keep them warm." The words were barely off his tongue when he got an idea. He'd send a fruit basket to their room at the Holiday Inn, with compliments of Louie Mo.

"What we shoot tomorrow? Action? Or big dialogue?"

"Running."

"Running?"

"I get in Dutch's trunk with the Steadicam and shoot you running. T-Rich matches your sneakers and Durbin shoots second unit, so I can cut in close-ups. We're almost there, man."

128

DOG BEACH

Running, thought Louie Mo. *Always running.* Troy's movie was beginning to feel like a reality program. *The Louie Mo Show.* Maybe he should never have come back to this house on the beach, this place so full of young, ridiculous dreaming.

15

RADAR LOVE

Dutch was driving back from Thousand Oaks at night, feeling oddly alone. She had gone to the baseball card dealer and offered to buy back the Super Bowl game ball. The dealer, a fish-eyed midget with bad skin, told her that he had sold it at a convention in San Diego almost two weeks ago, then he tried to push a rare Jason Banazak rookie card on her. What'd he take her for? she said. A fan of that Neanderthal rapist? Well, why the Christ did she want to buy the signed football, the midget parried. She didn't answer, just walked out, saying nothing.

Two doors down, she spotted a liquor store but walked away from it. A foot from her car, she changed her mind, went back to buy a bottle of Grey Goose. In the parking lot, she mixed a hefty portion in her water bottle with orange juice, poked a straw in, and drove off, sipping. A few emotional songs on the radio—"Rolling in the Deep" by Adele was one—and she felt herself going into that dangerous place of missing what once was. She switched from FM to CD and played her favorite ramp-up song, hoping to override her feelings.

> *I've been drivin' all night*
> *My hand's wet on the wheel;*
> *There's a voice in my head*
> *that drives my heel . . .*

Three years back, she was driving stunts for just about every production that came into Santa Fe. If it happened to be a Western, she stunt-doubled any female scripted into a saddle, but it was mostly driving for Everett Cook's bunch, the stunt unit nicknamed Team Extreme. Everett had worked with her dad, the much-respected precision driver Billy Wayne Dupree, one of the few stunt guys pulling down six figures a year. Dutch grew up around it, Daddy's little stuntgirl. After two daughters, Billy Wayne had hoped for a boy on the third go, but out came Debbie. He made her his boy just the same, and she loved it.

By the time she was eighteen, they were calling her Dutch and she was arguably the best driver on his team; she had a rep for being as tough and daring as her father, the man who had leapt off the cliff in *Butch Cassidy and the Sundance Kid*, although she could never remember if he had doubled Redford or Newman. He was gone now—dead from hard living—so she couldn't ask him. The stunt work had made him drink, and drinking made him ill. Illness put him out of work, which made him drink harder and die. That's when Dutch started drinking too. Tight-roping out onto that dangerous slope of alcohol that her father had dare-deviled and lost to.

It was on the set of an indie drama that she hooked up with a young wrangler named Keefe. By the end of the three-month shoot, they were talking marriage; Keefe had a dream of getting out of the movie biz, swearing off booze, and buying a small ranch. He thought she should get out too, while the going was good. Picture it, he said: the two of them spending their mornings making the hay rounds in the truck, drinking their coffees, and checking on newborn foals. It sounded idyllic to her, and boring as hell. He was waiting for her to get back to him on the marriage thing when the tragedy happened.

She'd been out late, slamming shooters with the stunt-boys and nearly missed morning call. They had all been telling stories about her dad and it got her emotional, drink-ing hard. She should have called in drunk, but that would have marked her forever. She tried to sober up, suck it up, drink black coffee all the way to the set in Gallisteo. When she heard that they were switching the stunt schedule and putting her Box 90 up first, she had felt a little panic, but she manned up. "Man up, little girl," Daddy used to say if he caught her second-guessing herself. She'd been doing drift-reverse 180s in her sleep since she was a teenager. She was Billy Wayne's hot pistol of a daughter; she peed diesel fuel, as the boys liked to joke.

Some on the set would go on to say that it was the stuntman on the dirt bike who fucked up the timing; most knew it was her. The guy, thirty-six with a pregnant wife, got hammered by the truck she was driving, slid under it, and traveled with the skid for a hundred yards before she even realized he was not on the other side, ramping onto the desert as scripted.

He was dead.

Dutch was fired. Fined. Blackballed from the drivers' association and tied up for months in criminal investigations and hearings. Every time she'd walk into the San Marcos Feed Bin now—her beloved Sunday-morning breakfast haunt—some wrangler or stunt guy would be in there and give her that look, even as they made nice. She had killed one of the fraternity, had shown up impaired. She had broken the sacred law that her father had upheld his whole storied career. Dutch had become a kind of leper chick, driving the lonely stretches between Santa Fe and Lamy, always followed by the ghost of a guy on a dirt bike. And always Keefe in his F-150, telling her to let it go and marry him, dang it.

Then came Louie Mo. All because Jen the makeup artist took mercy on her and invited her out to L.A. to chill. Didn't help that Crazy Jen was a party beast, the little house in Laurel Canyon always full of booze and blow. Jen had an older girlfriend who brought a guy over one night, a Chinese guy she'd worked with on a show long ago in Thailand. He was in town looking for movie work, she'd said. He was a quiet man, Louie, but after margaritas and weed, Dutch got him to open up about his stunt history. They traded stories all night and she found him to be hilarious, kind of sweet, and darkly mysterious. At one point, some buff actor dude had gotten a little out of hand with Jen. Louie had quietly followed the guy out onto the porch, moving in that youthful step, fluid as a cat. When he returned, everyone said, "Where'd that asshole Josh go?"

"In the car," Louie said.

It wasn't until the next morning that they'd discover the guy had been put through the windshield of his own Toyota, was sleeping off a beating and a hangover. Louie never said anything about it. He came in, sat brooding in a corner, and said he wanted to go home. But the costumer he had come with had left with Charles, and the displaced Hong Kong stuntman found himself buzzed and stranded in the Canyon.

Dutch drove him to Monterey Park—a long-ass haul during which they shared more stunt stories, lies, and easy silences—and they'd been a tandem ever since. It was the guys who sold blow to Jen who eventually made a loan shark gig available to the unemployed Louie Mo. A guy with fight skills could make a few bucks in any town. Louie just needed some wheels.

Feeling the vodka now, Dutch had that urge to put the hammer down. She was working the 405 South like the Daytona Speedway, deep in the zone. Maybe she'd just keep driving. Jump on the 1 with a few grand in her purse, head up the coast to Big Sur, maybe swing up through Calgary, find a real job where no one knew her name. Or maybe swing out and down, head back to Santa Fe, go look up Keefe. Better yet, she considered, she could just drive straight into the northbound traffic and call it a life. She kicked her sandal off. *Do it, Dutch,* she told herself.

> *We got a thing that's called radar love;*
> *We got a line in the sky.*
> *We got a thing that's called radar love . . .*

But then she thought of Louie Mo, making his stupid movie with the film geek kid, looking happier than she'd ever seen him—even if he was more physically broken than she'd ever remembered; he was pissing blood now, for Christ's sake.

She turned the wheels on the Chevy and got off at the Canyon exit, slowly, headed for Crazy Jen's place. She felt a little pride in not driving any farther with vodka in her blood. That was, at least, something. She'd finish off her Grey Goose and crash responsibly in her back room, sleep in; Troy was shooting nights for the next two days and she wasn't needed at the wheel until Thursday. Needed at the wheel; that was something too.

16

ANGEL TOWN

Hektor Garza was the kind of man that excited Zoe. Dangerous, irreverently tattooed, but not beyond making offerings to wooden folk saints and calling his mother on Sundays. Mostly though, it was the way he made other men roll over on their backs in his presence. She saw that, firsthand, when her father brought her to a business dinner one night at Boa Steakhouse (the one in Santa Monica, not Beverly), using her to ornament the table and bolster his reputation.

They had locked eyes that night, Zoe and Hektor Garza—the very night, she often reminded her father—that Hektor and his Guatemalan associates agreed to invest in *Slash*. "Stay away from him, Zo-Zo," Avi warned, before he could reel the words back in. He knew that forbidding her from a man would only make her want him all the more. Shit, he learned that when she was in seventh grade.

In bed, Hektor Garza was what Zoe called nasty. Sometimes too nasty, but only by degrees. On the second night that they slept together, he tried something that made her resolute in ending the relationship—she had even clawed his chest—but then his cell rang and he took a call from his mother.

From the bed she had watched him sit in a corner, moonlight on his mysterious tattoos, speaking in soothing Spanish to the woman he said lived in crippling pain. Then, only seconds after saying good-bye and kissing the cross on his necklace, he took an incoming call and said, in a terribly calm voice, "I have seen the Devil, on his knees. Begging to pleasure me in exchange for mercy. This is not a story, my friend; it is not some parable. I am an evil that exists outside any concept of darkness in your darkest fucking nightmares.

Pay my nephew by Monday or I will come see you." He had gently disconnected the call at that point, sat for a moment, looked at her, and said, "Do you want to get some ice cream?"

At the ice cream stand on Sunset, he confided that he was enchanted beyond reason by her beauty. That was fifty percent why he invested in Avi's movie and why he was now in trouble with his uncle Ortega Garza, who considered the investment risky.

Impulsive, even.

"What was the other fifty?" Zoe said.

"I love movies."

Zoe, sitting beside him, also licking Ben & Jerry's, looked up at him and swore she glimpsed the brown-eyed soul of a young boy. "For real?"

"I love movies. I want to be in the game. That's all."

"Well, you own a piece of an Avi Ghazaryan film. You're in the game now."

"Yeah," he said, but he sounded flustered. He was staring across the parking lot at some young guys just hanging out. Zoe felt herself tense. For a moment it seemed like he was going to get out of the car and confront the guys for no reason. Everything in his body language suggested it. Then he turned and kissed her, a vanilla ice cream kiss, and said, "Avi has given me a great opportunity. The American dream, you know? Does that sound . . ."

"No, no," Zoe said, "I know exactly what you mean."

"I mean, my mother's dying down there." He grew sullen again, kept looking in his rearview mirror as if he could see Guatemala in the night smog behind him. "So no mother-fucker is going to get in the way of my movie."

Zoe bit into her baby cone, let the wafer dissolve on her tongue. "What motherfucker would that be?"

"The director. The college kid."

"Troy?"

"I don't give a fuck what his name is. If he rips your father off, he rips me off. He rips off Ortega Garza. I swear to Saint Paulo, I'll cut his intestines out and make him watch."

"He's a filmmaker, Hektor. He's temperamental."

"Temperamental?" Hektor's face darkened and he turned a look on her that thawed her ice cream headache. "You have something going on with this guy?"

Zoe laughed, shook her head at such an accusation. "He's not my type. Not tall enough."

"I don't care if the motherfucker is as tall as that billboard up there. He doesn't turn the movie in next week, I'm cutting his legs out from under him. I've risked my ass on this. Everything. My whole family is watching to see how this turns out. 'Hektor's crazy movie investment.'"

He stared at her like he was going to strangle her with his belt. Then he broke into laughter, the most handsome smile she'd ever seen. He kissed her cheek gently. "Why am I telling you? That's not for you to worry about. You worry about your craft. Your craft, baby."

His cell rang again. He took a call from his nephew and spoke in quiet Spanish as he started driving back to his rented place in Studio City. She thought about her father warning her to "stay away from that bad actor."

That made everything all right again. That, and Hektor calling what she did a "craft."

• • •

Dutch was surprised to find no one home at the Laurel Canyon house. The front door was unlocked and ajar. The plasma TV in the living room was flickering silently with a Western movie.

Drunk for the first time in many months—and it hit her hard with painkillers still in her system—she navigated the course past the kitchen, saw no sign of Jen or Charles or any of the usual hair-and-makeup suspects who tended to gather at all hours.

She stopped in the living room and considered the silent TV for a long moment. The Western, she realized, was actually a gay porno rendition of *The Wild Bunch*. For some reason it semi-fascinated her and she drunkenly sank into the couch.

That's when she saw him.

Charles was on the carpet. His glasses were off and his head was damaged, blood everywhere. Blood on his half-buttoned purple shirt, blood on the leather couch she was sitting on. Blood on the walls like something out of *Helter Skelter*.

Dutch could not remember screaming in her life. Ever. Not even the time the accelerator on a stunt Camaro got stuck flat and she nosed into the side of the catering truck. She had merely whispered "Fuck," then lit a cigarette. Now she screamed. She screamed so loud they must've heard it up at the Hollywood Bowl.

Charles wasn't moving.

141

• • •

Driving back to her father's house in the Hills, Zoe texted, changed CDs, logged onto Facebook—posted even—and checked her e-mails. Twice she nearly rear-ended the same Audi. At a red light on Sunset, she saw an incoming e-mail from Troy Raskin. "See attached," it said. "Hope you like."

This was it, she surmised. The scene in which she blows Alexis to zombie pieces under the Santa Monica Pier.

Just as the light turned green, Zoe floored it, passed the Audi, and darted her way to King's Road and the winding ascent to Avi's house. Avi was out making deals, of course, so she let herself in and took an urgent pee in the downstairs bathroom, then hurried to her upstairs princess turret to check her computer.

With every echoing click of her strap-and-buckle riding boots up the staircase, the anticipation of gunning down the ginger bitch grew more heady. She sat down, undid the top button of her skinny jeans, and liberated a breath. The attachment from Troy was five script pages. But it wasn't *Slash*. A note above the script pages read:

Damn the Torpedoes, I'm Going for Broke.
Need You.

Zoe read the note twice, shook her head, bewildered. Then she started reading the pages.

• • •

Dutch stopped screaming when she heard a mewling on the bloodied carpet. Charles was gazing up at her, nearly blind without his glasses and blood matted at the bridge of his Romanian beak. She slid off the couch, tried not to move him. She noticed then that he was still gripping the TV remote.

"They hit me." Charles sounded like a first grader in the schoolyard, as if he merely had a bloody nose, not a hemorrhaging ear and mouth.

"Who?"

When he didn't answer, Dutch tried again, even as she dialed 911. "Who, Charles? Who hit you?"

"Pray to Jesus."

"*Who fucking* hit you?"

"Man said, 'Go with Jesus,'" Charles whimpered in confused agony, "pray to Jesus." He was fading in and out. Dutch heard the door open and she wheeled. For a moment, she thought the heat had showed up in record time, but it was Jen coming through the door with her makeup bags. First her crazy eyes went to the TV screen where a guy wearing nothing but chaps was getting it on with a Mexican saddle. Then she saw Charles bleeding on the carpet. She dropped her kit, screamed louder than Dutch had, and far more shrilly. She was still screaming and kicking in place when the LAPD *did* arrive.

In the chaos and crackling police radios, Dutch told a female cop what Charles had said. A guy hit him, said something about Jesus. Pray to Jesus, maybe. When Jen heard this, she whiplashed around and began screaming herself hoarse again. "Oh my God," she wailed. "It was them!" She kicked her legs again and Dutch tried to calm her as paramedics worked on Charles from all sides. "Those guys!" she screamed. "Those big guys from Mount Olympus. Those big guys from Mount Olympus."

The chick must be smoking crack, thought Dutch. Telling the cops that Zeus and Neptune had come down to lay a beating on the little Romanian hair stylist. But the female cop didn't seem to blink as she took the statement. Dutch realized then that Jen was talking neighborhoods, not Homer. Mount Olympus was a community bounded by Laurel Canyon Boulevard. "Those biker guys," she went on between breaths. "Fucking right-wing Christian motorcycle gang. They followed Charles home from the Roosterfish one time. They stuck a bumper sticker on his car."

The cops calmed Jen, got her to slow down, speak more

143

slowly. "Adam and Eve, not Adam and Steve," she said, describing the bumper sticker. But when the paramedics carted Charles's bloodied form toward the door, she collapsed in hysterics again and began wailing his name.

"Who lives here?" the female cop kept saying, unruffled by it all. Dutch noticed that the lady cop, too, had bags under her eyes. If Charles wasn't half-unconscious he probably would have advised the cop to ice them. One of the white-gloved paramedics was telling Jen that Charles was going to be okay, that the bleeding appeared worse than the damage. Was he a hemophiliac? Was he HIV positive?

Jen kept shaking her head no as she wept, but she seemed uncertain. Lost. Dutch felt some guilty relief. Not just hearing that Charles was going to live, but that the beating was possibly a hate crime, or maybe related to some kind of L.A. sex play Charles had gotten himself entangled in. *Not* anything to do with her and the getaway-driver lifestyle Charles had warned her about.

She hurried for the door, caught up to the gurney at the ambulance. The paramedics kept her back, but she managed to get a hand onto Charles's arm. "You're going to be okay," she told him, but he had an oxygen mask on and was unresponsive.

"Whose car is that?"

A black cop near the curb was asking the question a few feet away from the parked Chevy. Then a radio call came in, distracted him. Dutch could hear Jen still weeping like a little girl inside. Dogs were barking from the house next door. Sirens were coming and going.

DOG BEACH

Suddenly exhausted, Dutch made her way to the front porch and sat down. She fished out a smoke, lit it. Just let it all pass, like a bad dream. That's what she told herself. Bad dream. And when it passed, she knew what her next move would be. Pack up her shit and move on from Laurel Canyon. Just in the event it wasn't Bikers for the Bible or the hammer of the gods; just in the event it was the curse of Dutch Dupree, following her like that ghost in the desert.

17

DAY FOR NIGHT

Zoe was crying, mascara all a mess.

"You're my father, and all this time I didn't have a clue?" Her top lip quivered like she was trying to fight an ironic smile. "You just show up after twenty years and I'm supposed to be, like, yo, Dad, hello?"

She was half-lit in halogen, sitting in a shuttered-up Malibu bait shack, facing a stern-faced Louie Mo. "How do I even know you're who you say you are? It's all been one big lie. And now I should forgive you?"

Louie stared hard at her, but it was impossible to meet her gaze. He searched for the words in English, sweat at his brow, then said, "Line."

"I only tried to protect you," Troy fed the dialogue from the shadows.

"Only I try to protect you," Louie said, a bit wooden.

"Okay, cut," Troy said, springing to his sneakers. "Nice, Zee. Really nice."

She was playing Cho's twenty-one-year-old daughter on meeting her estranged father for the first time in a remote shack. Troy had told her in his e-mail that he wanted to cast her in the role—she had a great ethnic look and was the right age—but the film was a secret project, a labor of passion. "Classified stuff, Zee," he wrote in the e-mail.

She had called him back within ten minutes, said she loved it. This was no run-around, tits-bouncing zombie crap; it was a real scene, she said, a chance to really act, and great material for her reel. But something more was happening out here near Point Dume, late at night, just her, Troy, Louie, and a silent, focused T-Rich, who was lighting and shooting the scene with the 435.

"I want you to try it again," Troy said, sitting at the back wall near the halogen lamps. "This time, I want you to think about your own father."

"You think I haven't been?" she said.

"No, I know you have. Just own it more. Real stuff."

"Real stuff . . ."

"When you say, 'How do I even know you're who you say you are?,' I want you to see Avi and his BMW, his breakfasts at the Polo Lounge, the big house in the Hills. Is he who everyone thinks he is? Are all his houses really paid for?"

T-Rich eased his eye back from the camera and tried not to be too obvious in looking at Troy. Louie just sat there, firm in his role of Cho the outcast.

"Has your father," said Troy, "created a web of lies that's

endangered people you might care about, even if you really don't know you care about them?"

"What the fuck are you even saying?"

"One simple thing: Has he lied to his daughter about who he really is? And are you in deep, fucked-up denial?"

Zoe just stared at him as he went back to his director's seat behind the camera. "That's all I'm saying."

They shot the scene again, and this time she began to improvise, going off-script and, at one point, breaking into cold laughter that was unexpected—and perfect. When Troy called cut, he went to her, kneeled beside her, and gently gripped her arm.

When she looked up, tears dirty on a cheek, she saw that Louie Mo had welled up himself. Just from her reading. In fact, he had to leave his seat on an old lobster trap and go outside.

"I know what my deal is," Zoe said, her eyes pooled. "But what's up with him?"

Troy watched through a small window as Louie limped, hunched, toward the moonlit surf. "Might have something to do with why he wanted me to change the son character to a daughter. Only note he gave."

For a moment Zoe almost felt something for the broken-down stuntman she hardly knew. While she'd been drawing on her relationship with her real father, maybe the guy, Louie, had been playing to a child he hadn't seen since leaving China or Japan or wherever he was from.

More than that, she felt something for Troy, who brought

149

raw emotion out of them both. Maybe he *was* a director to watch, like so many had said when he came out of film school. Maybe he *was* wasting his talent on her father's high-concept pics.

As for Troy, he felt he had learned something about Avi that had been haunting his sleep ever since the night Zoe came to his bedroom; she had said her father felt Troy could make a low-budget film look like twenty mill. That had stayed with him. It had landed as a compliment but took root as something foreboding.

"How'd we do, T-Rich?" Troy said, standing up and stretching.

"Beautiful shot, man. The light, the wild track, everything."

"Nice work."

Louie Mo was back, his eyes clear now. He stood in the doorway of the little bait shop and said, "Martini shot?"

"Martini," Troy said. Then he looked at Zoe. "You have another one in you?"

She straightened her back, flipped her hair off a shoulder. "How about you, Louie?"

Louie looked at her and knew what she meant, knew she had picked up on some buried feelings. He nodded and took his seat on the old lobster trap.

"Rolling," Troy said. "And sound . . ."

• • •

Later that night, Troy and Zoe sat on the bar patio at Moonshadows, cooling down after the shoot. They were drinking

"What about you?"

"What *about* me?"

"You wrote the shit, Troy. Where'd it come from?"

"Where'd it come from?"

Zoe studied his eyes in the candlelight, could see he was feeling the eighty-eight proof. "Little NYU rich boy, what do you know about broken souls and abandonment and all that shit?"

"You want to know the truth?"

Zoe bit delicately into the gin-soaked cucumber, waiting on his answer.

"I got it from a movie called *The Gunfighter*. Gregory Peck, directed by Henry King. You ever see it? It was part of this Western noir thing going on in the early fifties. Kind of weird. But kind of cool."

"So your life's just a mash-up?"

"What kind of rude question is that?"

"I don't think you borrowed that emotion from a Gregory Peck movie." She leaned closer, took his cucumber, and dipped it in her drink. "My father does have you wrong, doesn't he?"

"About the shit I do best, you mean?"

"No, about you being some rich film-school brat. He thinks that if you fail, your mommy will bail you out. Pay him back his investment."

Troy shrugged but lowered his eyes. Zoe caught it. "You know who else was in that movie?" Troy said. "Karl Malden. I always find it unsettling when fucking Karl Malden shows up in one of these—"

"Troy, you don't have any safety net, do you?"

Hendricks martinis and talking about her scene, which takes they thought were keepers.

Troy had never had a martini before, but after his third beer, Zoe had dared him. "If you're going to be a player," she said, "you need to upgrade from keg party fare." Hemingway drank gin, she footnoted.

"How do you know about Hemingway?" Troy said.

The insult was so blatant that Zoe smiled, incredulous. "Actually, he drank Gordon's. But if he were alive today? He'd be a Hendricks man."

"And where'd you get that from, *Midnight in Paris*?"

"UC Santa Barbara. Before I dropped out." She took a sip and said, "Didn't want college to fuck up my education."

"So, this is what?" Troy said, feeling his head begin to birl. "Just gin and vermouth?"

"Vermouth?" Zoe said. "Hemingway would never commit that sin on a perfectly good martini."

Troy flagged down the waiter and ordered two more.

"Easy there, big guy," she warned.

When the fresh drinks arrived, Troy raised his, made a toast to the night's work. Zoe clinked her glass off his.

"So . . . is this my only scene?" she said. "The bait shack?"

"Yeah, but it's the money scene. I mean on an emotional level."

"You really pulled some stuff out of me, I guess."

Troy sipped, content in the moment. He ditched the cucumber from his drink, breathed in the surf air. "Louie Mo had it going on too, didn't he? I mean, as much as a stunt guy can."

"Of course not."

"What about your mother in Connecticut?"

Troy took another sip of the extra-dry gin; his third Hendricks was now close to spent.

"Why is it," he said, "that whenever people hear Connecticut they always assume you're from Greenwich or Darien, or someplace. I mean, does everyone from Tennessee play the fucking banjo?" Troy drained the martini then looked over his shoulder toward the men's room line. He excused himself, a bit unsteady on his sneakers.

• • •

Zoe found him down on the beach, relieving himself behind a cement pylon and singing something that sounded like Coldplay. Normally, he'd get a shy kidney, but for some reason he felt comfortable with her standing there. Mostly because the gin had taken the edge off.

"Compact and portable," Zoe said. "Hate you guys."

Troy tried to get past her, told her he needed to go pay the bill.

"I took care of it," she said.

"I do have a mother in Connecticut," he said, hardly realizing that they were walking north toward the lights at the Point. Zoe was feeling the drinks, but Troy was downright wobbly. "She's the youngest daughter of Grand Duchess Anastasia Nikolaevna of Russia."

"Get out."

"That's what she thinks anyway. She's been in an institution since I was eleven."

"For real."

"When she first started seeing Freemason code in postage stamps, my father freaked out. He ran away from her when I was six. I went to live with my uncle Ronnie. That would be Bridgeport, not Westport."

It was in an apartment above Harbor Video, he confided, where he spent most of his childhood and teens, surrounded by movies, watching compulsively. Other than school, he rarely left "the vault," as Uncle Ronnie called it. Yet, he felt like he was traveling constantly, entering movie worlds where characters became like family. He spent his childhood backtracking those films to their sources. Started with Spielberg and Lucas and worked his way back to Howard Hawks and John Sturges, to the spaghetti Westerns of Leone, films inspired by the masterworks of Kurosawa. He told Zoe about the excitement he'd felt when he discovered—just by studying Kurosawa's use of telephoto lenses, depth of field, and mise-en-scène—that the Japanese director had, in fact, been influenced by John Ford Westerns. He'd sit there for hours, inserting and ejecting and cross referencing. He devoured flicks by Italian B-movie directors with the same insatiable appetite with which he downloaded, in his mind, every shot from every Shaw Brothers movie to come out of Hong Kong in the '60s and '70s. Over time, Uncle Ronnie even stopped using the computer to catalog and check DVDs; he'd just ask Troy.

When he was seventeen, watching movies was no longer enough; he hungered to make his own. He used his entire four-thousand-dollar savings to make an HD short on the sordid docks of Bridgeport; it got him into NYU. So did the completed screenplay that would become the template for his bachelor's thesis—the heist film called *Game Clock*. The Austin Fest brought him to the attention of Avi Ghazaryan, and now here he was, walking on Las Flores Beach with the producer's daughter, baring his drunken soul. He didn't realize, until he was done, that he was holding her hand. She was carrying her heels in her other, which made him suddenly aware that his sneakers were soaked and he didn't care.

"Hey," Zoe said, "you're not that short after all."

"Not with your eight-inch heels off," Troy said. She laughed as they strolled on, Troy seeming to sink into another thought.

"The guy with the dolphins," he said. "When he went up to Alaska, do you think he knew? You think he knew he was feeding himself to the bears?"

"Let's get you home," she said. "You've got to finish your movie."

"Which one?"

"*Your* movie, Troy."

Troy dug for his keys. Zoe told him they were going to walk to Dog House and he could jog back for his car in the morning. He turned a defensive look on her, clutched his keys in his fist. "I am perfectly capable of driving into a cement mixer," he proclaimed. Then he surrendered his keys.

At the house, she saw him inside, but they both hesitated when they found someone asleep on the couch. It was Dutch the stunt driver, out cold. She had Louie's white denim jacket tucked at her chin like a blanket. Troy and Zoe

stared at her like she was a stray cat for a second then moved
to the bedroom, where Zoe helped him out of his salty-wet
sneakers and socks.

"I love you," he said, with all the conviction of a frat
house drunk. Zoe laughed, tucked him in, and left.

18

WAGES OF FEAR

That Sunday they drove—Dutch, Louie, and Troy—way the hell out to Irvine to see an effects guy Dutch knew from the fringe. After meeting him at a warehouse—and Troy writing a fat check from the Dog House Productions account—they were driving back toward Malibu with a trunkful of explosives. Louie didn't say a word as Dutch maintained a careful, steady forty miles per hour in the slow lane.

"This is totally *Le Salaire de la peur*," Troy said from the backseat, as if afraid his volume might trigger the explosives.

"You speaking French back there?" Dutch said. "You're making me horny."

"*Wages of Fear*," Troy translated. "French thriller from 1953. Ever see it?"

Neither Dutch nor Louie responded.

"Classic. These dudes have to transport nitroglycerine through a mountain pass in South America. You feel like they're going to blow sky high at any second."

"How you know all these movie?" Louie said, watching the freeway ahead.

Dutch weighed in, stern: "There's a hundred and ten pounds of demolition charges in the trunk. We get rear-ended, even a little fender bender, we blow up the 405."

"Don't worry," Louie said.

Something about Louie Mo taking charge put Troy at ease. He asked him then if it was true that he had doubled Jackie Chan a few times but never got credit for it. There was a rumor, Troy said, that it was really Louie Mo who slid down a pole through shattering glass in *Police Story*.

"Boys together," Louie said.

"What do you mean, 'boys together'?"

"Peking Opera School."

"Opera school?" Dutch chortled. "You never told me you were a singer."

"No," Troy volunteered. "He's talking about *Chinese* opera. Acrobatics and weaponry and shit."

"That's right," Louie said. "In same school, orphan boys: Jackie, Sammo Hung, Yuen Biao, Corey Yuen, Yuen Wah, Yuen Tak, Little Tai."

"The Seven Little Fortunes," Troy said.

"How you know so much?"

"They all left the school to become stuntmen," Troy said. "Jackie and Sammo became action stars. The others just did stunts, right? The Seven Little Fortunes."

"Eight," Louie said, almost as if lost in a memory. "Eight boys."

"Wait a minute," Troy said. "You saying that the Seven Little Fortunes were actually eight?"

Louie confirmed with a crafty silence.

"*Dude.*" Troy sat up. "You're like the fifth Beatle. That is so cool."

"Youngest, me. Always I jump from the highest places, make everyone laugh. I did a lot of stunt for the famous ones. Sometimes no credit. Not good to make star lose face, you see."

"What the fuck are you guys talking about?" Dutch said.

"That's why this is so freaking cool, Louie," Troy said. "The Eighth Little Fortune gets his due."

"I know."

Dutch laughed quietly and mimicked the lack of modesty. "I know."

Louie looked at her, offended, but her eyes had darted to the rearview, so he swung a look at the road behind, his eyes narrowing. Troy caught the look, turned full, and saw the black van following.

"Go fast," Louie said.

Troy slunk down. "She can't, man. We'll blow."

Dutch lowered her window, signaled for the van to pass. Instead, it hugged her bumper. "Do you know who this is?" Dutch said.

Louie shook his head, but his body said differently. Troy saw it; Dutch saw it too. "All right," she said, steeling herself. She kicked her right sandal off, adjusted her seat. "You want to play chicken, bud?"

159

She monkey-toed the gas pedal and rocketed forward, coming up fast on a phone company truck. The van stayed with her, its windshield opaque. A foot from the truck bumper, Dutch cut the wheel and swung into a fast lane. Horns blasted and brakes pealed, but Dutch began jumping lanes, picking up speed.

Troy slid lower in the backseat, not breathing. He could see the black van hovering, tailing like a road-rager. Dutch hit ninety, jumped to the outside lane, and gunned it. When brake lights lit up before her, she swerved back to a middle lane, narrowly breaching a gap in the skidding traffic.

"Jesus," Troy yelled. "You're going to blow us the fuck up."

"Speak French, why don't you?" she said, roaring toward the slow lane and a confounding exit, half-blocked by construction signs and dead road machines. The van made the adjustment, stayed with her.

"Who are these guys?" she said.

Troy winced; bad timing for a movie quote, even if her father did double either Redford or Newman on *Butch and Sundance*. But then he realized she was serious, and rightfully so; she couldn't shake them, so she grabbed her E-brake and yanked. The Chevy skid sideways toward the exit; Troy almost puked. Flying at them now: a construction sign and white dust. The van kept going but was forced to stay with the southbound traffic, blaring a fitful horn.

The exit ramp came up like a cement floor hitting a drunk in the chin, then it doglegged back around. Troy closed his eyes; he could hear rubber shrieking and Louie making short, emphatic breaths in Cantonese, fully aware of the explosives in the caboose. Then they came to a stop.

"Asshole," Dutch said, her eyes on the rearview mirror. She was sweating. Unusual for Dutch.

"Who was it?" Troy said. "Somebody you know?"

"In Los Angeles," Louie said, "so many dangerous people. They are hijacking all the time, right on the highway."

"Carjacking, you mean," Troy said, still trying to breathe. He could see Dutch's attractive eyes in the rearview mirror and noted that they'd gone from hazel to a shade of green. Glassy green.

"Okay," she said. "That was a hard nine."

"What you mean?"

"On a scale of one to ten. Cortisol speedball."

Troy didn't respond. He was feeling a strange lilt in his gut, not unlike what he used to feel at NYU when he'd cross Washington Square Park and have a close encounter with a mentally ill bag lady. Something was off here, something that fucked with the rules of normalcy. Dutch had told him, that night over sushi, that Louie had fallen on his head from great heights one time too many, had a few screws loose. Now he was wondering just how many, just how loose. And her, those eyes as glassy and tranquil as a heroin addict after a fix—that was weird shit.

"We'll go back through the Canyon," Dutch said.

"Nice," Troy said, imagining another three hours of hairpin turns and cortisol speedballs.

• • •

Banazak was walking his lapdog along the yacht basin on Fiji Way, his eyes hidden by a visor and sunglasses. He had an iPod in and was listening to classic vinyl. He loved new stuff like Government Mule, but when he really wanted to feel motivated, it was '80s rock 'n' roll. Van Halen could make him bench four hundred pounds on a good morning; Molly Hatchet could rock his deadlift off the charts. But this was his rest day and he was walking easy. Not that he wasn't vigilant; he was always keeping an eye out for the lesbian couple who walked a large Doberman. His only fear in life was of something happening to Captain Jack, his tiny apso.

His cell phone vibrated in his pink shorts and he slapped for it a bit awkwardly, overeager to take the call. When he checked the caller ID, he was even more eager.

"S'up, Paps?"

"Another call on the Chevy," the former private eye to the stars said on the other end. "PCH. Malibu, between Dukes and Moonshadows."

"On it," Banazak said. He hung up, took a breath. He began to jog with purpose.

• • •

He located the Chevy right where Papagallo said, pulled in, and left a car length between them. He wanted some space to make an ID on the chink, and some ramp-up room so he could blindside him with the baseball bat. The guy wasn't going to get a chance to throw any karate or slip off behind a passing train. Banazak had him in a perfect position, would ideally beat him between the parked cars and the beach house gates, where no one could really get a glimpse. Some movie star—Banazak imagined Cher for some reason—would come out to her Mercedes and find a dead Chinese man.

Sitting there, like a duck hunter in a blind, Banazak rolled down his windows and slid his seat back half a foot to give his massive legs some room. In defensive football, they used to talk about the fine line between patience and overplaying the ball. Timing took years, but when it clicked, it was like bulldogging or spearing a fish. Fast, brutal, done. That's how he was going to blitz this rice monkey, make him beg. He wondered if it was possible to beat a man so force-fully that dental records would be moot. He even wondered if there was wisdom in flinging the guy out into the PCH traffic after rendering him disabled. Then no one would even know he'd been clobbered. Maybe get Papagallo to get some blow-job queen to call 911 and report a drunk Chinese guy walking down the middle of PCH. Whatever.

Then a car pulled in, oddly abrupt. The silver Lexus with rental plates nosed even with the Chevy, reversed into a smooth parallel-park job. In three seconds it was perfectly tight between Banazak's SUV and the target vehicle.

"Fucking asshole," Banazak said. There were four guys in the car, all business. He felt his 'roid rage quicken as he waited for them to get out, but they remained seated. A few moments later, however, one of them opened a rear door. Slowly, he climbed out from the backseat. The guy was Asian and dumpy, dressed in a plain suit. He took a few idle steps, looked around at the addresses on the gates, then lit a cigarette.

Banazak studied him; he didn't look like his mark. Had

to be some connection, though. He caught a side profile of the driver, saw that he was Asian too. They all were. No, you didn't have to be Sherlock Holmes to smell something fishy. And the way they were loitering, it seemed they were waiting for someone. Then the cigarette smoker looked directly at him, did a double take. He seemed surprised that someone was behind the wheel of the parked SUV; it almost made him jump. He stared for a time, smoking and squinting. The brazen eye contact did something to Banazak, made him get out. Fuck patience.

"Where is he?" he said, coming at the Chinese guy so aggressively that it made him scuff a step in alarm. "Where the fuck is he?"

"Sorry, my English not so good."

Banazak went to the driver's side of the Lexus and leaned in, inspecting each face. The driver was a stout guy with a red tie. The one in the passenger seat had an expensive coif of layers like some sporty chick and wore tiny sunglasses.

"Where's your boy?" he said.

"Pardon?" said the passenger, his voice silky and British inflected.

"Which house is he in?"

"Why you are so angry?"

Banazak hiked a knee into the door with a bang, made all the men flinch. He put his face right in the driver's, nearly fogging his glasses with his breath. "I'll kill every fucking one of you little nip motherfuckers."

Then he shoved the driver's head back against his seat. "English not so good?"

DOG BEACH

The passenger said something in Cantonese. The driver kept his head back, held it still. The passenger raised a small handgun and fired two shots, both punching into the big man's chest. Banazak rocked back half a step then pitched forward against the car. Tiger Eye fired a third shot, piercing Banazak's forehead. The huge man tried to fall in at them through the window, but his steps were carrying him northward, out near the traffic. Still, he kept on, shuffling toward his SUV now as if to go fetch the baseball bat. The four Chinese men watched him, fascinated. The big *laowai* was still alive with a bullet through his brain, staggering like a headless chicken at a Mong Kok market. He grabbed for his door then spun and slid hard. Buckling, he went still against his front tire, his eyes fixed toward the sun.

The Lexus eased out, drove away.

19

DEADLINE HOLLYWOOD

Avi sits at the Coffee Bean, the one at Sunset Plaza, looking at the trades on his phone, scrolling down through Deadline Hollywood's *announcement blurbs:*

— *CBS Buys Gay Father Comedy*

— *MPAA's Chris Dodd Urges Tech Community to Support Ban on Rogue Websites*

— *Damon, Affleck to reunite for new Lehane Beantowner*

— *Paramount proceeds with* **Caution**; *Cursio and Ellison to Pen Mo-Cap Actioner Based on Crosswalk Signal*

Avi nearly spits out his espresso, scrolls back up. He reads only the opening line of the article and says, loud enough to reach every sidewalk table around him, "Tyler, you snaky little motherfucker. I'll sue your ass and I'll sue fucking Brad Gray—I'll own the studio."

That's when he notices the guys getting out of the Hummer at the curb. Central Americans, five of them. Hektor walks at the front, quick and certain. Guns come up. A woman screams as—

BULLETS RIP INTO AVI GHAZARYAN, shredding his sport coat, throwing him violently from his chair. He tries to crawl toward the walls as chairs tip all around him, SAME WOMAN SCREAMING. Then, on his elbows, in pooling blood, he sees the back door of the Hummer open, white shoes step down. The guy walks calmly across the bloody plaza and trains an AR-15 on him. Avi looks up and recognizes the man as HARVEY KEITEL.

"You are a lying, scamming, scum-of-the-earth cocksucker," Harvey says. "Amateur hour is over." Then he UNLOADS. Avi feels himself jackhammered off the concrete in a death spasm. Still, he gets up on his elbows, looks right at the Central Americans and Harvey Keitel and says, "I'll fucking sue you." And he dies.

In death—

• • •

Avi woke up. It was a cool, late morning in the Hills. He had slept in, compliments of a double dosage of Lunesta. Despite the slightly metallic taste on his tongue, he had needed it. But those dreams? Terrible. Violent. And what was up with Harvey Keitel? Maybe it had something to do with the doomed financing of an independent film that he had once tried to attach Keitel to. He had used the term "amateur hour" back then, when he walked out of a meeting on Avi. Must've stuck in his mind.

With his kettle heating up and his medium-bold coffee in the Bodum, he did his stretches. As was his routine, he checked his iPhone as he loosened his quads, leg up on a chair. There, on the front page of the L.A. *Times* online edition, he saw it:

Ex-NFL Star Slain on Malibu Highway

A football photo of Jason Banazak in younger, healthier years appeared just below. Avi read a little of it, felt a kind of chill. Maybe he had picked up on the murder vibe and had the violent dream about gunshots. Ridiculous, he thought; he was starting to sound like his daughter, Zoe, when she'd go off about energy and chakras and all that New Age crap. There was a far more pressing article about the Euro and its impact on the U.S. economy just adjacent. If he had read on, he would have learned that the murder, in broad daylight, occurred less than a hundred yards down from the beach property he was renting to Troy and his film brat friends. He might have even worried about his daughter, the way she liked to sunbathe on Las Flores and go in and out of the house at will.

Avi poured hot water into the press. He was still feeling the nightmare—feeling the bullets—which was a good thing. After dreams like that, he didn't feel so unlucky. Espe-

169

cially when drive-by stuff actually happens, like to the football player on PCH.

As his coffee brewed, he stood in front of the wall calendar, did his shoulder rotations, and got his bearings. Troy had eight days to deliver a cut. Eight days. If he didn't, maybe that Coffee Bean massacre dream would come true. But if anyone was taking the heat, it was going to be Troy. Avi had trusted him, let him live in his house with all his little freeloading buddies.

He dialed Troy, was surprised how quickly the kid answered.

"I just want to say, you little motherfucker, you don't have my cut in eight days, I can no longer hold back the wolves. What you have is a clusterfuck. Unreleasable. Your second act is like the Bataan Death March. Fix it. I can no longer hold back the sharks. Eight fucking days, Troy, you little Jew motherfucker."

He hung up and felt good. His coffee was ready. The first cup, always full of such promise.

• • •

"That was random," Troy said, hanging up just as Durbin came out of his bedroom. "He was talking like he saw my cut or something. He even called it a clusterfuck."

"At least you guys are on the same page," said Malone.

"Dog House–gate," said T-Rich. "We been hacked."

"Dude," Durbin said, holding up his iPad. "You see this? Murder on PCH this morning, right outside."

"I heard the sirens, thought it was an accident."

"No, check it out. Nine thirty in the morning, this Oakland Raiders guy was gunned down, just down the road from Gary's."

"You shitting me?"

"No. That's, like, right outside our front door."

Malone was already on it, reading his phone. "Steroids," he said with that stoner grin. "Guy had a history of steroids, drug busts, date rape. I bet it was a drive-by. Lucky we weren't hit."

The Dogs were on the case. T-Rich stepped outside, came back with the paper. "They got the yellow tape all along the road. CSI."

While Durbin and Malone hurried with juvenile zeal to investigate, T-Rich opened his iPad on the table where Louie and Dutch were eating cereal. "Shot three times," T-Rich said. "Point-blank. Sick."

Dutch craned to look then choked a bit on her Puffins. Louie gently patted her back. "You see that, Louie?" she said.

"Football player was shot this morning, right outside."

"Outside where? Here?"

"Yeah."

She slid the paper where he could see it, the photo of a younger Banazak. Louie pulled it closer, looked harder.

"What, you like the Raiders, Louie?" T-Rich laughed.

Louie stared at the photo then looked over at Dutch. Her eyes said it all: It was him, the big steroid head who they'd subcontracted to and then ripped off. What had he been doing just outside the house where they were crashing? Had he been relentlessly tracking Louie Mo since the encounter

171

in Monterey Park? More important, who put three bullets in him?

The way Dutch was looking at Louie, he felt like the accused. Then he wondered if maybe Dutch, who had finished off her bottle of vodka in the night, might have plugged the guy with her little .22 sidearm when she went out to her car for smokes. She did hate the guy for being a rapist. If not one of them, then who? Guanyin, goddess of mercy?

"All right, peeps," Troy announced. "Big day. Let's go get it."

Dutch looked back at the iPad. T-Rich was already on his email. Life was cheap up here, she thought, on the golden side of the overpass.

172　　Louie shook an oxy like dice, then threw it back with a swig of orange juice. "Let's go get it."

But Dutch could read Louie, could see he was disturbed; like something beyond his control was closing in.

20

CITY ON FLAME

Tiger Eye was the only one of the Triads not talking. There were nine of them now—five of their San Francisco members coming down out of respect—all sitting at a shitty table in a small pizza joint in Playa del Rey. They spoke in clipped Cantonese about the big crazy guy who had attacked them and paid the price for it. Louie Mo must have protection, they reasoned.

The sworn brothers from San Fran didn't wear business suits like the Hong Kong faction; they wore a mix of hip black leather jackets and tracksuits. One of them, a crew-cut guy almost as tall as Yao Ming, wore a lightweight, gray linen duster.

While they chattered and laughed in their southern Chinese, Tiger Eye was staring at his iPhone, scrolling through the attachment that his hacker in Hong Kong had just sent. No longer could they stake out the Las Flores beach house and hope to kill Louie Mo coming or going. They'd have to find another location.

The overseas hacker used the American filmmaker's e-mail address to poach his password and get into his account. From there, he uploaded a shooting schedule with maps of locations, even driving directions. It appeared, Tiger Eye told the sworn brothers, that Louie and the kid were down to just a few more shots on their calendar. They knew where to find him now. They knew when. It would be a hit and run, and a night flight back to Hong Kong. Tiger Eye couldn't wait. He hated the laziness of Los Angeles.

INT. NUMBER 9 BAR—NIGHT

174   As the club empties, CHO gets his duffel bag and walks over to a tired BUZZ. He offers him some cash.

                  CHO
        That's for the mirror.

                 BUZZ
        Screw the mirror. It made me look
        heavy around the middle anyway.

Still, Buzz takes the cash. Just the way he is.

             BUZZ (CONT'D)
        You better get out of here, Cho.

DOG BEACH

                    BUZZ (MORE)
They're coming for you. Nowhere
left to run, my man. No more
time . . .

                    CHO
You've got yourself a nice place.
Good feng shui.

Buzz smiles. Cho lingers for a second more,
looks at the Elvis clock behind the bar, hefts
the duffel, and starts out with Wes.

The BLIND MAN listens to Cho's footsteps.
Lifts the sax to his lips and PLAYS an end
to the night riff. A theme of sorts. We will
call it THE CAGE SONG.

                    • • •

Louie was back in the beach house after shooting half a day
in the crappy Venice bar Troy used as the Number 9 Bar.
The crew went off to shoot Dutch burning rubber in a parking lot so Louie had a rare afternoon to himself. On his way
to his upstairs room, something caught his eye in the hallway
water closet: a vintage clawfoot bathtub that had been tempting him for weeks. None of the boys ever used it, and Louie
himself only showered in the tight stall in his bedroom bath.
But now the fine tub beckoned.

He filled it with a mix of hot and cold—mostly hot—got in, and savored the warm soak all the way up to his neck. With a skylight overhead and European prints on the walls, he felt like Ringo Chou must have when he starred in his movies: like a king. He lit a cigar that T-Rich had given him one night in Zuma, a nice Dominican, the kid said it was.

He let the smoke out slow and easy, sank a little deeper, feeling his hips loosen. It was the most peaceful moment he had felt in years. Then he heard a dog barking. The sound was a common one in Las Flores—they called it Dog Beach for a reason—but this sharp yapping seemed to be coming from the little private walkway where the boys kept the trash barrels and Malone kept all manner of surfboards and kayaks.

176 When the barking finally stopped, Louie relaxed again and began practicing his lines at a whisper. He was trying to remember that direction Troy always gave him: Keep it simple, keep it real. He remembered the first day that Troy said, "Keep it stupid, simple," as some kind of joke, and he didn't get it and had grown offended. That was the same day that Louie had executed a spinning heel kick and Troy called it "ridiculous." The director had to chase Louie down, explaining that the word was actually high praise. Perhaps the worst offense was when Malone told Louie that he was "the bomb." Over time, Louie began to get a better feel for the Dogs' lingo and humor and he often fired it back at them, followed by a sophomoric chest bump. He was smiling at the memory of one of those exchanges, savoring the cigar, when that dog began barking again. For ten minutes straight it yapped.

Louie toweled off, pulled on his red sweat-suit bottoms,

and made his way downstairs. The barking was so loud and sharp down near the living room that he wondered if a dog had gotten inside the house. Then he spotted it. The small white dog was on the back porch, snapping so close to the glass on the French doors that it looked like he might smash his teeth.

When Louie approached, the dog grew quiet for a moment, staring at him with deep-set eyes. It growled, then resumed its yapping in near hysterics. It struck Louie then that he had seen that dog, heard that shrill yelp somewhere before. When it became clear, the blood rushed to his face. It was Banazak's lapdog, the little apso from the houseboat in Marina del Rey. A dead man's dog.

What the hell was he doing here?

All Louie could figure was that when the former football pro was gunned down on PCH, the dog must've jumped out of his SUV; amazing that it hadn't been pulverized in the traffic. No, it must've taken off scared along the side of the highway, found its way down to the beach, and wandered lost for days before ending up on the porch of Troy's house. *But why?* Did he sense that Louie was in there hiding? A month or so ago, he had scented Louie's intentions on the houseboat and threatened to bite him. It was as if he had sniffed Louie out now and was trying to alert passersby.

Some women strolling by laughed and kept turning to watch the resolute little puffball yap up a storm. A guy throwing a tennis ball to his own dog was staring too. Louie had no choice. He opened the French doors and let the dog in. It hesitated for a second then entered, nosing its way around the living room.

"Bad dog," Louie said to it, not sure what else to say. "You don't come to this place, like this."

The apso sniffed at Louie's favorite shabby-chic chair, picked up a scent, then did the unthinkable. He lifted his back leg and pissed a tawny spot into the clean white fabric. When Louie made a move toward it, it began barking aggressively.

This was a disaster of no small proportion. If anyone was looking for the dead man's dog—if anyone spotted it here where Louie Mo was staying—all kinds of questions would be raised.

Louie had to do something quickly. He looked around the kitchen and considered the trash compactor. Bad idea. If Dutch were there, they could've put the dog in the trunk and drove him fifty miles north and let him out in a parking lot. By the time she got back from the shoot, though, it might be too late; the LAPD could be crawling all over the property.

With the apso nosing at Troy's pile of dirty clothes near the laundry room, Louie looked out the French doors. The guy throwing the tennis ball to his retriever was now a good distance down the beach. North and south, the coast was clear.

Louie picked up a pizza crust from the counter and approached the dog. He lowered himself onto his haunches and made the offering. The dog sniffed then gently took the crust. It tried to carry it off to a corner, but Louie scooped the animal up. "Nice boy," he said.

Louie carried the lapdog out onto the porch and down to the beach. He hurried to the ocean, looking each way

again. Wading into the surf, Louie moved beyond the out-
cropping of large shoal rocks until he was waist-deep. He
couldn't believe he was doing this, but he could see no
other way.

He tossed the apso into the sea. It paddled desperately at
first, making small piglike sounds, but then it began to falter.
It was not a swimming dog like the Labs and goldens that
dominated the beach. The dog began to sink, just its muzzle
above water, whining now.

Louie waded back to the shore, discreetly looking up
and down the beach. Ankle-deep, he turned and saw the dog
still making an effort to stay above the waves. It lurched and
pawed and tried to swim, but even then it was turned the
wrong way, headed toward Catalina.

"Fuck," Louie said. He looked back at the house, plowed
a hand through his wet hair. Then he jogged back to the
surf. He waded in, dove, began to swim out to the dog. It
was about to go under for one final time when he reached
it, seized it by the scruff. Clutching the dog to his chest, he
waded back to shore. He heard the voice then, a familiar one.

"What do you think you're doing?"

The redheaded girl stood there in her shorts and pink
Uggs, her eyes hidden behind large sunglasses. "Did you just
throw that dog into the ocean? Were you trying to drown it?"

"No, no," Louie said. "Salt water cleans out the skin, very
good for breathing. This we do in China."

"Drown-the-dog tai chi? Dude, you were trying to . . ."

She lowered her sunglasses and stared over the rims with
a horrified look. She seemed to be making some kind of

connection now. "China? Wait a minute. Were you going to . . . were you going to *eat* him?"

"No, he's my dog. I told you. Cold bath."

Alexis was backing away from him, shaking her head in slow disgust. "I'm sorry, that is wrong. That is just . . . so fucking wrong."

She turned abruptly and walked away, still shaking her head. She spun and yelled something back at him, sounded like she was crying in dismay. With more people coming down the beach now, Louie took the shivering dog and walked quickly back to the house. The sun was going down. . . .

· · ·

"Magic hour," Troy said from behind the Arri. "We're going to catch it. Damn, we're going to get this light."

T-Rich, Durbin, and Malone all stood by in the Zuma Beach parking area watching Dutch roar out of the distance in the Chevy. Zoe was there too, sitting in a set chair in large sunglasses. "Like fucking Garbo," Durbin had whispered to Troy. Avi's daughter had recorded a wild track earlier in the day and had decided to stick around. "Troy," she said now, a bit nervous. "Car's coming too fast."

"I trust her," Troy said. "She's a pro."

Dutch approached at high speed, did that E-brake thing that was her specialty, and carved a one-hundred-yard skid that threw Malone's carefully placed Pyrolite into a spray—all of it backlit in the last two seconds before the sun sank behind palm trees. The car careened toward the camera, Troy tempting fate behind it. If Dutch had been William

Tell, Troy was the guy with the apple on his head; four feet away, the Chevy came to a screeching rest.

"Sweetness," Malone said, the crew clapping. When they ran video playback it looked even better. Troy bumped knuckles with the Dogs and high-fived an aloof Dutch, and then, turning to Zoe as she came out of the chair, he kissed her. It startled them both for a second, then they locked in a gaze. "That's a wrap," he said, still eye to eye with the Armenian beauty.

"Brewski's at Trancas?" Malone summoned.

"Meet you there," Troy said.

• • •

In Dog House, the place unlit, Troy and Zoe were kissing even as he unlocked the side entrance. They knocked over Malone's longboard from where it leaned, tipped Durbin's *Lord of the Rings* trivia game, upended the mounted production strip-board near Troy's desk; urgently they made it to the bedroom.

181

Troy remembered how Zoe had once unzipped that tiny mocha dress; he knew right where to probe and yank. Damn, he had rehearsed it a million times in his head during many an inappropriate moment. When she tugged at the belt straps on his baggy Jams, they sank hard to the floor, the pockets weighted with lenses and compressed air. In seconds they were in bed kissing like the house was burning down and they didn't care.

For all of Alexis Cain's reverse cowgirl and porn queen vocabulary, it couldn't hold a candle to what was happening with Zoe Ghazaryan. Only once did a film reference run through his mind, but he shared it with her at a whisper and she liked it: "*From Here to fucking Eternity* wasn't this hot," he said.

It lasted no longer than four minutes, but it was her who came first, him a half-beat behind. They lay there, breathing hard together and laughing at the craziness of the moment.

Then a dog began barking, pushed at the unlatched door, and entered. Zoe covered herself quickly, Troy sat up, alarmed. Louie Mo appeared and gathered the little Lhasa apso in his arms. It kept barking at Troy and the girl like they were breaking and entering. "Sorry," Louie said.

"Louie, what the fuck?"

"I didn't know you come home."

"What's with the dog?"

"Mine."

"What do you mean 'mine'?"

"He's my friend."

"Dude, Avi has a no-pets rule; you can't bring a dog in here."

Zoe giggled from under the sheet that covered her face up to her eyes. "He's adorable. Is that a little cockapoo?"

"I can't get into any more shit with Avi. We better call animal control, or the police—"

"No," Louie almost yelled.

"What do you mean 'no'?"

Louie hesitated, looked at the wet animal, and said, "I love him." He was holding the dog close to his chest even as it snarled with disdain, and Louie didn't seem to demonstrate much affection in return. He backed tentatively out of the room, gently closed the door with his foot. Troy fell back on his pillows, rolled his eyes toward the ceiling. Zoe rested her head on him and laughed some more. "I'm sure my father has a No-Hong-Kong-stuntmen-living-upstairs rule too," she said. "Let the dog stay."

21

THE ABBY SINGER

Avi sat at the Coffee Bean on Sunset, reading a script that had placed in the finals of the Garden State Screenplay Competition. Nothing went better with the first few sips of strong espresso than opening a brand-new script by a young fresh voice. One never knew. Until he got to page four, of course. By page four one always knows. That was another Avi law.

Now at page three, he knew where it was going: right into the trash can on his way to his car; fuck page four. This kid from the Garden State was destined to work a tollbooth on the turnpike. That said, Avi made a mental note to borrow one of the detective characters for his own found-footage concept called *Illegal Aliens* about extraterrestrials crossing the border and taking over a South Texas hamlet. He closed the script, looked up, and saw Hektor Garza sitting across from him. The Guatemalan was wearing the same blazer he wore to the Ivy two months back, and his hands were folded on the table in controlled anger. Avi stared him down.

"What's with the fucking look?" Avi said. Inside, he was unnerved by the guy, but he knew how to counter that, how to play social jujitsu. It was an Avi trick that he had even taught his daughter long ago when she was self-conscious about the weight she had gained in her ass. "Each time you run into someone you know," he counseled her, "before they can comment, ask them *first* if they gained a few pounds, and tell them that it truly suits them." It would completely reverse the tables and send the potential offending bitch into a tailspin. It worked like gangbusters.

Now, he did a variation of the technique on Hektor Garza. "You piss me off, Hektor," he said. "You want to be a player, you have to know the fucking game."

Hektor was thrown for only a moment. Then he reddened.

"Hey, man. Fuck you. The deadline is now. It's in the contract, man. You show me the finished movie."

"There is no finished movie." Hektor stared back at Avi through his dark glasses then looked around, seemingly taking stock of witnesses to whatever crime he might commit right there. "The kid ripped us off," Avi said.

"Even after you sent some muscle to the beach house?"

Avi nodded. "He's been living in my place like a Malibu prince, off your money. And you know what he's doing? Making his own fucking movie."

"I've had it with this schoolboy. Does he even know who invested in this thing? Does he know who he's screwing with?"

"He's got a rich mother in Connecticut. He was raised

with the silver spoon. Entitled. Like all of them. Like all of these little pricks."

Avi punctuated this by handing the script he'd been reading to an old Hispanic man wiping down tables. "Could you put this in the men's room? To conserve toilet paper."

Yes, nodded the confused but dutiful old man, taking the script in due course to the men's room. "Hektor, my friend," Avi said, taking his final sip of black magic. "This game is about risk. This kind of movie can either break the bank or bleed you. There is no completion bond. No insurance. Just like life."

"I've got too much skin in this one, Avi. You guaranteed me."

"No. Our director did. He guaranteed us all."

"That's just not acceptable, man."

"There is another course," Avi said, looking off across the street. "I fire him. We begin the search for a new director. Could take a few months, it could—"

"A few fucking months?" Coffee drinkers were turning and looking, but Hektor didn't care. "Even if the movie came out next week, I'm still a year from seeing a return. My uncle gave me six months to make this work."

"Only one out of one hundred thoroughbred horses has the potential to be a race champion. The rest are good for shit."

"But you told me this kid was the next Orson Welles."

"An ironic prophecy, isn't it?"

Hektor didn't know what that meant, and Avi knew he didn't know what that meant but knew he wouldn't out himself as a film dolt. "We've all lost skin on this one," Avi said, already walking to the curb with his Beamer keys out.

Hektor looked at his phone. Three incoming calls had been made by his uncle Ortega Garza, no voice mail. Hektor looked over at a scruffy guy in sweat clothes and sunglasses, talking on a cell and writing on an iPad. Some forty-something pretender, pretending he was in the game. Like everyone else.

Hektor was no pretender. He didn't play games. By sunset today, he was going to make that clear.

• • •

Malone walked onto the Venice set, his red hair tousled, his eyes hidden behind black sunglasses. When Troy spotted him, he left his Arri on its stand, went to see him. "How'd you do?"

"The Malone Zone has been established," the effects man said. "It's all rigged in a delay pattern. I wrapped the lower columns in chicken wire so nothing lands in the fallout zone."

"So this thing's really going to explode?"

"No. It's going to *implode*. The top floors and gravity will pancake the lower half of the building. I laced a chlorine donor in the upper walls. You'll get some flame. Gonna be sick."

"Nice," Troy said, looking back to see if Louie and Dutch were getting into position for the next shot. "You sure there's no squatters or prostitutes or anybody living in there?"

"None. It's so fucking condemned, there's not even rats."

"Fire department?"

"All we have to do is give them twenty-four hours so they can circle the wagons, just be there. City's stoked to get rid of that fire trap, on a movie company's dollar."

"Excellent."

"What shot is this?"

"Abby Singer," Troy said, using movie set slang for the second to last shot.

Troy and Malone watched Dutch get behind the wheel while Louie gingerly crawled onto the hood, lay on his side, and gripped a windshield wiper. He made some joke about taking a nap while Durbin checked the light meter.

"After the car hits Louie," Troy said, "he hangs on to the hood through the streets of Chinatown."

"Then he grabs on to a passing bus, that the shot?"

"I cut the passing bus. Now he climbs into the car through the passenger side and beats the fuck out of the driver."

"Sweet."

"He kicks the driver out of the moving car and takes the wheel. That's how he gets to the old building for the money shot."

Malone grinned, hiked up his baggy shorts, and watched Troy take his 435 off the camera stand. There had been some discussion with T-Rich about whether to shoot a handheld POV shot with the HD or with the Arri, sped up to 21fps. The Arri won out; this was a shot that called for real film, dirty and raw.

Troy climbed into the backseat, propped the camera on his knees. Dutch started to light a smoke when Troy stopped her. Then he reconsidered. "Yeah, okay, let's go with the smoke."

Dutch flicked her lighter. Louie rapped on the windshield as if to say, "I'm aging over here, let's get this shot."

Troy fished out his radio, spoke to T-Rich. "When I call action, shoot the reverse on the chaser cars. Over."

"Got it," T-Rich crackled over the radio. "Over."

"Durbin, lock it up," Troy said. Dutch gave him a nod in the rearview. He checked his camera then brought the radio to his lips. "We're rolling. And . . . *action*."

Dutch goosed the pedal. Louie lurched on the hood, gripping a wiper blade. "Good, Dutch," Troy said as he filmed. "Hold that speed, we're looking good."

Louie clung to the moving car like a pro, lifting his chin so the wind caught his hair, the camera his profile. It wasn't that he was mugging; he played the harrowing moment calm as a cat. Earlier that day he had proposed the idea that Dutch hit her washer fluid and spray him so that he was forced to slip and slide. Troy nixed the idea, felt it was too cute. Louie then suggested that the car have gasoline in the fluid sprayer and that the driver then toss a lit cigar onto the hood and he would do a full-burn in motion. When Troy nixed that, Louie seemed almost relieved. He just liked getting creative, being a part of the vision. At the end of the day, Louie thought, favoring the American expression, a clean shot on the hood of the moving car best served the movie.

Now T-Rich came across the radio and said, "I got the chaser cars getting lost, but there's still one on your ass."

"There's not supposed to be one on our ass," Troy said, working both camera and radio. "We lose all three cars, remember?"

"Yeah, but this is a fourth car. Did you set up a black van?"

Dutch's eyes hit the rearview, then the side mirror. "Shit," she said. "It's that fucking stalker."

Troy spoke calmly into the radio: "Durbin, did you lock up the street?"

"I did, man, but that van came out of a side street and almost hit Malone."

Louie did his belly crawl onto the windshield while Troy kept filming, even as he strained a look over his shoulder. The van hovered, mirage-like, just as it had weeks earlier on the 405. Like the driverless truck in Spielberg's first movie, it seemed to have a demonic life of its own.

"It's tagging us," Dutch said.

"Just keep driving; we're rolling."

The wind ripped at Louie as he did his painstaking crawl to the window. For a moment, Troy could see the pain showing in the stuntman's jowls as he gripped the side mirror and window frame, began to pull himself in, legs first. Troy shot the white sneakers, the clean Levi's, Louie lowering himself into the passenger seat then chambering his left leg for a kick toward the driver. "Just hold that leg like that, Louie," Troy directed. And then the rear windshield exploded. Glass rained like diamonds over Troy, down the back of his shirt. "What the fuck!"

"They're shooting at us," Dutch said.

"Malone Zone?" Louie said.

"No," Troy screamed, burrowing low with his camera. "Someone's shooting, man."

Another shot punched the trunk of the Chevy and Dutch flattened the accelerator. "Hang tight."

Louie turned sideways, squinted at the shadowing van. "Not Malone?"

"Not fucking Malone!" Troy yelled from down near the floor. He wasn't sure if he'd been shot or not. Cold glass shards made his back feel wet, and his eardrums felt punched-in, damaged.

Louie slid lower, planted his sneakers on the floor to brace himself. Dutch read their position in the side mirror, scoped out the intersection ahead as the light turned yellow. "We're running this bitch; hold on."

Troy set the camera safely on the floor, grabbed for his radio. He wanted to radio Durbin, have him notify the cops. When he said as much, both Louie and Dutch reprimanded him. "No cops," Louie said. It didn't matter; radio was out of range.

The Chevy careened into a strip mall, forcing the van to wait for oncoming traffic. Dutch shot across the tiny parking area and out a side-street exit, scraping the muffler as she punched fuel. As she raced toward an intersection that would kick them onto the 5, Louie turned around — first to look for the stalker, then to examine Troy.

"You okay?"

Troy carefully pulled himself up, tugging at his shirt and

letting the glass crystals shake out. A few stuck to the sweat on his back, but he was certain now that he had not been hit. Still, he was shaking all over. Dutch moved her eyes from the rearview to the side mirror and back to the street. She had skillfully lost the chaser and was now just three blocks from the on-ramp.

"That black van was on our ass last week, on the 405," Troy said. "I take it they're not the paparazzi."

When no one responded, Troy smacked the front seat. "Who the fuck is after us? Talk to me!"

Louie angled a look on Troy now but said nothing.

"I wanted to call the cops," Troy said. "You said no. Why? You enjoying the goddamn rush? The cortisol whatever?"

"Come on, Troy," Dutch said. "Until your movie, Louie was breaking knees for a living and I've got some driver's license issues. Can't have cops opening up a can of worms."

"So who's after us? You going to tell me it's one of your ex-wives?"

"Bad people," Louie said. "They want to kill Louie Mo."

"What?"

"I leave Hong Kong, okay?" Louie said. "They don't know where I am. Now they do, okay? Because of you. Because of stupid kung fu movie."

"You mean the Chinese investors?"

"In Hong Kong they have other name." Troy stared at the back of Louie's head, waiting. He said it first in Cantonese, then in English. Troy knew the lingo; he'd seen enough Hong Kong action movies to know the name of China's underground criminal society.

"Where am I going now, Troy?" Louie said. "Australia?"

Troy sat back, numb. "Triads," he said under a dry breath. The wind was raking at his hair through the blown-out rear windscreen, yet he didn't seem to feel it. Interstate 5 did not lead to Australia, but wherever they were heading was a lot safer than going back to Dog Beach.

"Rebecca Lo," Louie finally said, out of nowhere. Then he answered Troy's question from two weeks earlier. Whatever happened to her, that hot chick from *City on Flame*?

Louie told Troy and Dutch about that night in Victoria Harbor, the "Burning Boat," Rebecca's beautiful face carved up like a smiling clown. And he told them what he did after he found her like that and rode in the ambulance with her to the hospital, holding her hand all the way. . . .

• • •

Just before dawn at the Take One karaoke bar in Kowloon, Louie is drinking with the stunt team. They are laughing, reenacting the burning mast gag, telling stories from the past. Like always after a big stunt, they are decompressing by getting outrageously drunk. They laugh, they cry, they sing. Gambei!

But not Louie, not tonight. He just sits and drinks in deep silence, thinking about Rebecca over at the hospital in her fourth hour of surgery. It could take more than one hundred stitches, they said. He left out of respect for her family.

Tommy Zhang, the youngest stuntman, comes to the table. He pulls up a chair beside Louie Mo, the big brother to the stunt players. Louie drapes an arm around him, pours him a glass of red wine. In breathless Cantonese Tommy Zhang whispers to Louie, tells him to look over at the bar. Louie's own face goes crimson. He spots one of Uncle Seven's young underlings, a motorcycle-riding member of the 49. Cao, his hair coiffed in layered feathers like a bird. When he sees Louie looking at him, he does something taunting. He lifts his glass of grain alcohol and does a little "Gambei," as if to say, we are watching you.

Louie's chair scrapes to the wall as he abandons it and he crosses the bar. The younger stunt team can only watch as Louie goes to the bar, plants an elbow beside young Cao. "Why they hurt her? Why? She didn't work today. Or yesterday."

"That was for you," Cao says. "You don't feel pain, so what good is it to beat on your stupid ass?" Cao took a sip of courage then looked Louie right in the face. "Whenever you look at her, remember who you made lose face."

"You should have killed me."

"Uncle Seven is taking out a life insurance policy on you. As one of his stuntmen. Otherwise, your death is shit."

None of it makes sense to Louie. He had always worked well with the Triads who controlled the industry, but this new breed has no honor. No discipline. Everything ugly about it shows in Cao's face. He is almost pretty for a man but with eyes as cold as a Beijing winter. Cao is barely a member of the 49, still merely what the Triads call a Blue Paper Lantern Boy.

Louie looks away in disgust, then pivots hard with a palm strike, driving Cao's glass into his face. It hits and shatters at an angle that instantly destroys his eye. Blood everywhere,

*grain alcohol burning in the ruined socket. Louie kicks him
so brutally in the chest he clears three bar stools, hits the la-
dies' room door, and keeps going, sliding on his bloody cheek
over jade-colored tiles wet with piss. Screams of agony echo
as men scramble to help, or run. Louie sets down some Hong
Kong money on the bar and walks out, not too fast, but not
too slow, either.*

*He has no choice now but to get out of Hong Kong. He
will take the ferry to Macau, catch a flight to the mainland.
He wishes he could see his two-year-old daughter one last time,
but Uncle Seven never knew he had a child and he wouldn't
lead him there now. Never endanger her. Straight to the airport he goes, considers destinations on the departure monitor.
London? Rome? Barcelona . . . ?*

*That's when the running began. Twenty years ago. And it
hadn't stopped yet. . . .*

• • •

Dutch thought she had heard every story from Louie's past,
but she had never heard about his final, violent night in
Hong Kong. She knew about the ex-wives—the Two-Headed
Dragon—she even knew about a few Fujian girls he slept
with at the boardinghouse in Monterey Park, but she never
knew about the tragic, unrequited love in Louie Mo's crazy
life. Or how he came to run adrift in Los Angeles.

Troy ticked off a list of Rebecca Lo films with both an
expertise and an appreciation that moved Louie. When Troy
remarked that she was "kick-ass" and had amazing fight skills,
Louie tamed a bittersweet laugh in his throat. "Dancer," he

said. "I taught her wushu moves so she looks like, you know, good fighting. But her kung fu was very ugly. Dancer only."

"So these guys," Troy said, getting to the real matter at hand. "They saw my YouTube post and posed as investors to try to find you?"

"No pose," Louie said. "Triads invest. Maybe they would still invest, but still kill me. Do you see? Take life insurance on me too."

"This is crazy," Troy said. "I mean, beyond crazy. This is . . . you have to get the fuck out of L.A."

"And go where?"

"I don't know. Australia, like you said. New Zealand or some fucking place. Can't let them find you, man."

"One thing first," Louie said. "We finish the movie."

"Forget it, Louie," Dutch said. "It's over."

"We get the martini shot, then it's over."

"You've had too many concussions," Dutch said, flustered. "You can't make a responsible decision right now."

"This boy," Louie said, jerking his chin toward the backseat. "He give everything for this movie. He's just starting. He's in trouble with his boss. Me, I'm done. We finish the movie."

Dutch looked at Troy in the rearview. His hands were gripping the old, bulky 35 millimeter like a security blanket, hugging it to his chest. He met Dutch's hazel-green eyes.

"A-all right," he said, assuming his director's voice even as he stammered. "Let's get over to the last set, grab the shot, and get the fuck out."

"We can head for the desert," Dutch said. "Vegas. Get lost there a few days while he figures out where to go."

Louie nodded, watched Dutch signal and head for the exit. They were north of Chinatown, and so was the black van, not visible again until it pulled off the exit with them. Whoever was following was damn good at it. . . .

22

THE MARTINI

The condemned apartment building was off the 110, in a bankrupt region between L.A. and Pasadena. Looming beyond a patchwork of abandoned warehouses and fenced-in fields of dirt, it was a perfect location for a tense climax. Better still, it was a structure crying out for a merciful death; it needed to be blown off the landscape and the city didn't have the funding to do it itself. Malone prepared the ritual; Troy was ready to do the honors. Louie Mo was ready to pull the biggest stunt of his almost storied career and then get the hell out of Southern California.

Approaching in the Chevy, they looked up at the shell of the building and the defunct, rusting construction crane nearly touching it on the far side. Troy monitored the light. "Didn't plan it this way, but we're going to catch the magic hour."

Indeed, the sun was lowering behind the freeway. Louie

opened the glove box, dug in around the empty pill vials and his metal nunchakus. He removed something that looked like a TV remote. For a moment, the car went still.

"I do this so many times, so long ago," Louie said. "You radio me, Troy. Tell me when rolling. I run, set the red button. Thirty seconds, I come out other side. Make the jump."

"I'm going to shoot from the bridge, Louie."

"Like in the storyboard."

"That's right."

Louie popped up the collar on his white denim, started to get out. He looked back at Troy and said, "Old school."

He was nearly out of the car when the black van growled up alongside, making him freeze. Troy ducked low, convinced now that this was a demon car; even the driver's window was tinted and opaque.

Dutch swore, started the ignition, but two guys appeared at her window—must have come out the rear doors of the van—and one had a small knife at her cheek.

"Shut it down, lady."

He was short but pit-bull made; so was the other one, both Latino, both showing goldwork in their teeth. Now three more spilled from the van to cover Louie's side, one had a firearm. Still another, a guy who looked more Native American than Latino, wrenched open Troy's door and said, "All of you, out, out, out."

As several more spilled out of the black van, it reminded Troy of *Nanook of the North*, when that impossibly small kayak keeps pouring out an endless number of Eskimo passengers. Only these guys weren't Eskimos; they were the Los

Angeles chapter of some Guatemalan gang, likely the ones that Zoe once alluded to.

Stepping away from the Chevy, Louie was fully expecting to face off with Hong Kong enforcers, but instead, he found himself flanked by three swarthy Latinos, two of them now armed with handguns.

"You want me?" Louie said, maintaining a neutral stance. "I go."

"Why would we want you, Kato?" said the one without a gun. He was tall and unfairly handsome for a guy who drove such a piece-of-crap van. Wearing a vest over a naked torso, he was all tattoos, his intimidating body a mural of snakes and colored roses and fanged goat skulls. Before Louie could make sense of the demand, the Indian-looking guy on his left slung Troy hard against the van. Troy made a pathetic whimper that sounded to Louie like "ow" or "whoa" and the stuntman spun into a ready stance. Then he saw the gun at the back of Troy's neck. The kid looked terrified. Dutch was ordered out of the car by the gold-toothed pair, and she obeyed, looking toward Louie for some kind of logic.

"Who are these people?" Louie said.

"I don't know." Troy was trying to see the Mayan gunmen at his back.

"I'll tell you who," Hektor said, strolling to the rear of the Chevy and taking a seat on the trunk like he owned it. His dark eyes drilled into the young man. "We're investors in a movie. You know which one I mean?"

"Yeah," Troy said. "I think so."

"You think so?" Hektor said something in Spanish and

the Mayan took Troy's chin in his hand. Louie made a move, but a gun waved at him from near the van.

"Maybe you think you can rip off Avi, you little poser, but do you know who put up two million in cash?"

"Two million in cash?" Troy said.

"Don't play fucking stupid, schoolboy."

Dutch and Louie notched a gaze over the hood of the Chevy; three minutes ago they were racing to get Louie away from the Hong Kong Triad, now they were being ambushed by some Los Angeles gangbangers who only wanted Troy and were talking about two million in cash. Louie was feeling a concussion migraine coming on. Dutch was feeling claustrophobic. She kept looking at the wheel of the Chevy and plotting a fast lunge, an escape route. One of her reverse 180s could spin them toward the rusted bridge if she had even a whisper of a gap.

Hektor spoke Spanish again and the Mayan released Troy's chin, hard. "I know about your mother in Connecticut," Hektor said. "She's going to wire me my money, or get a UPS box on her porch, two-day air. Guess what will be inside the fucking box?"

"Leave this boy alone," Louie said.

"Shut the fuck up, old man," Hektor said, sliding off the trunk and stabbing a finger toward the Asian.

"You got scammed," Troy said, and everyone looked his way.

"At least he fucking admits it," Hektor said, giving a bewildered laugh, but still fuming. "He *admits* it."

"Not by me, man," Troy said. "All I did was try to make

a piece-of-shit zombie movie look decent on a shoestring budget."

"How about I put a fucking shoestring around your little fucking neck, *chivato*? You think two million in cash is shoestring?"

"Two mill is fucking *Avatar* to me, okay?" Troy said, sweat soaking the hoody under his leather jacket. "But I didn't see no two mill. I didn't see the investment from the Albanian guys in New York either, or the co-prod money from the indie music dudes in Alhambra with the sucky soundtrack."

"What do you mean you didn't *see* it?"

"Avi had investors pool millions together. But all he gave me was one hundred and eighty grand to go make the movie, make it look like twenty mill, so you and the other investors would be satisfied. You'd feel like producers. Get your name in the credits at the end, then make a fat return. Right?"

Hektor said nothing, just sat back on the trunk of the Chevy, his brow knitted as he did the math. Louie squinted, felt like he had lost all command of the English language.

"While Avi walks away with what—four, five million in cash that never made it onto the screen. It was a *scam*, bro. You got scammed. *I* got scammed. Who knows how many cold calls he made to people with a hard-on to see their names on a real movie starring Eddie Morales?"

"You playing games with me?" Hektor said. "Do I look like a mark to you?"

He walked toward Troy now, seemed much taller up

203

close. "You know what we do to posers like you in Guatemala?" He was staring point-blank at Troy now. "We cut their heads off with a dull knife."

Now they heard the sound of tires slow-crunching gravel on the old industrial road leading in. The silver Lexus was followed by a bigger, darker car. The Central Americans appeared nervous, speaking urgent Spanish as they tried to discreetly conceal their weapons while still keeping Troy under heat.

When the Lexus pulled up and parked a dozen yards distant, Hektor angled a glance, hands on his hips. "You know who this is?"

"Yeah," Troy said but offered no more.

Out of the Lexus stepped four Chinese business professionals, the driver wearing bifocals. The passenger, Tiger Eye Cao, showed something like relief on his face when he saw Louie Mo standing at the center of the gathering. Five more Asian men wearing leather jackets and tracksuits, and a tall, crew-cut one in a long linen duster, got out of the other car.

In Cantonese, Tiger Eye said, "Nice to see you, Mo Chen Liu. So many people back in Hong Kong miss you and send regards."

"You got old, Cao," Louie said in the Hong Kong tongue. "Like me."

Tiger Eye shrugged. "Men grow old. Pearls grow yellow. There is no cure." Then he smiled and said, in refined English, "But rock and roll never forgets."

Hektor darted his eyes between the Chinese speakers. "What's with the fucking board meeting here?"

"You want Louie Mo?" Troy said suddenly, taking a brazen step toward the Chinese men. "You'll have to get past his vanguard."

Troy knew the Hong Kong lingo. "Vanguard" was a challenging word, traced back to the very roots of secret societies like the Triad. In Shaw Brothers movies it usually precipitated kung fu brawls, a myriad of swords.

"Do you even know who these guys are?" he kept going, now that he had them rapt. "They'll put your heads in a fucking UPS box and send it to your mothers!"

Troy was screaming it now and both the Guatemalans and the Triads were looking at him, confused. So was Louie, even as he translated Troy's words into shouts of Cantonese. Tiger Eye slowly removed his expensive shades. That amber gemstone of an eye stared straight ahead as the other crept over the Central American crew; he could see the Mayan holding a 9 mm pistol alongside his leg. The guy was inching it into position.

Tiger Eye said one word, guttural and clipped.

The tall, crew-cut Triad member opened his linen duster and swung up a 12-gauge, sawed-off Browning. He fired on the two Guatemalans near Dutch, smashing skin and bone. Dutch dove through the open driver's-side door of the Chevy, squirreling low.

Hektor pulled an open-bolt firearm from his waistband and ducked behind the car, using it as a shield as he fired at the Asian crew. Louie ran through a squall of gunfire, grabbed Troy, and flung him toward the open rear door.

"Go!" he yelled as he rolled over the hood of the Chevy, trying to throw a cyclone kick. Instead, he landed ungracefully on bloody gravel. One of the gangbangers was lying, bladder-shot, by the tire, trying to stay low as bullets riveted the side of the black van; return loads shattered the windshield of the rented Lexus.

Louie rolled over gravel, came up on the crew-cut giant from an angle that allowed him to steal the man's centerline. He slapped a hard *pak sao* downward and in, stripping him of the sawed-off weapon before crushing his rib cage with a knee. As the guy toppled, Louie ran over him, using his face for traction. He could see—in his periphery—Tiger Eye trying to look at both him and the Latino gunners.

Tiger Eye defied the gunfire and set up for a shot on the running Louie Mo. He had him dead to rights until a bullet clipped the hem of his suit jacket, grazing his flesh. It was Hektor, firing his Glock over the roof of the parked Chevy. Tiger Eye fired back, smashing the rear passenger window. Hektor wasn't sure if he was hit by shards of glass or gunfire. "Bitch," he cursed, dropping low and grabbing for a fresh magazine. Nausea flooded his insides for a second and he stopped to check his wounded triceps. He had good cover behind the car, but now it screeched away, throwing gravel and fishtailing. It was plowing right toward the Chinese. Hektor aimed to shoot the driver in the back of her head, but he quickly checked down; why stop a missile headed at the enemy?

Quick on their feet, the Chinese crew avoided being run over and kept firing at the Angelinos in what sounded to Troy, low on the backseat, like news footage: more like flat, popping reports than booming firepower. It wasn't a movie; it was real.

Tiger Eye was up on a knee, his suit jacket bloodied but unrumpled. The big, crew-cut shotgunner was up again too, crouched nearby. They both located Louie Mo, moving at a dead run for the condemned building. All they had to do was finish off his protection, these tattooed Puerto Ricans or whatever they were, swearing in Spanish with every round of gunfire; so fucking dramatic, thought Tiger Eye. Again, he spoke quiet Cantonese and the big Asian shed his duster, came up with a piece of Croatian hardware. With the calm bearing of a Zen archer, he unloaded the machine pistol at the van, shredding its side and keeping the last three survivors pinned down. They didn't stay there long. Running out together, they fired and yelled, then went down just as quickly, all but the Mayan, who rolled under the van. The big Asian's machine pistol strafed the other two like it did the van's sliding door.

On the far side of the van, Hektor, bleeding near his goat tattoo, crawled against the bald rear tire and gripped his handgun at his knees. Who the fuck did this kid Troy have on his side? he wondered. North Korea?

• • •

Louie dashed across the open first floor of the abandoned building, his footsteps throwing echoes back at him as he made his way to the stairwell. He had been in this dump a week earlier, blocking out the money scene with Troy. He knew the only way to the top floor was up the stairs, but it had taken him fifteen minutes to make the climb during the scout; now he'd have to run it. Passing a cement column, he saw how Malone had wrapped it in chicken wire and Geo-Tech, knew that the explosives were packed deep inside. The scent of a hot blowtorch was still lingering in the dark space and so was a pungent trace of Malone's weed.

Just as Louie reached the stairwell door where someone had long ago spray-painted his second-favorite English word, gunfire split the air, echoing from twenty directions. He heard a bullet ring off rusted pipes, and he worried for a moment about the C-4 set in linear-shaped charges on the support beams. Another gun blast—sounded like the big guy's shotgun—slammed into Sheetrock a foot from Louie's left shoulder as he lowered it and bulled through the door.

• • •

He bounded up the first flight of steps, trying not to think about his hip going out on him, but he could hear footsteps scuffling in the pitch-dark behind him. In the stairwell leading to the third floor, he caught his breath, looked up at the next towering flight. No way could he scale this one and not be overtaken by Tiger Eye's boys. How many were there now, anyway? He saw two go down, mortally hit. Six, he guessed.

DOG BEACH

Louie went through the third-floor door, glanced up, and assessed a tangle of exposed pipe and insulation. He leapt high enough to catch a cold pipe with his right hand and pull himself up, his knees balled high. When a San Fran Triad in a black leather jacket tripped through the door, breathing hard, Louie dropped and double heel–kicked him, sending him back into Tiger Eye and two more shooters bringing up the rear. A stray gunshot popped; Cantonese cursing echoed.

Louie landed and lunged to mount the third-floor stairs, but somehow Tiger Eye had scrambled up behind him. Maybe it was vengeance for twenty years back, but he was breathing with an animal determination, aiming his heater at Louie's head. He said something in English, sounded like "You good to die, bitch" or "You took my eye, bitch."

Didn't matter; Louie dropped as the gunshot hit the metal stairs. He put his weight on his hands and leg-swept the Triad, at the same time drawing the metal nunchaku from his back pocket. He snapped the weapon outward, trying to hit Tiger Eye's gun arm. Instead, he hit the gun itself, smashing fingers with it. When it fell, Louie inverted the nunchucks and stabbed for the solar plexus. Tiger Eye blocked the attack and fired a combination that Louie recognized as advanced Wing Chun. He could tell, instantly, that the man practiced routinely on the traditional *mook jong* wooden dummy. But as Louie always liked to say, wooden dummies don't hit back. He snatched an incoming strike at the wrist, cleared it, and punched Tiger Eye

209

in the face. Nothing fancy. Tiger Eye stumbled sideways. Louie pivoted, shot out a round kick. He purposely landed it where he saw blood on Tiger Eye's jacket. As Tiger Eye went down, Louie was already clearing three steps at a time, bolting upward.

The big Yao Ming look-alike in the linen duster filled the doorway now, took aim with his Croatian pistol. Two feet from the next door up, bullets flogged metal and Sheetrock.

Louie stormed the gap, sprinting up to the fourth floor, limping toward the fifth. Three more floors up, the walls and crossbeams would be rigged with extra canisters, packed thick with C-4 and RDX, for dramatic effect. He was almost there, almost in the Malone Zone . . .

210

• • •

On the old industrial bridge outside, Dutch eased off the gas. There were no guardrails and no water in the canal below, just ugly cement, a patina of dead algae. No one was chasing them now; the gunfight down in the gravel fallout zone had left several men severely wounded, if not dead. The survivors among the businesslike Triads had pursued Louie into the abandoned building. Any remaining gunfire was coming from within, hollow and erratic.

Troy was still flat on the backseat, eyes skyward, trying to breathe. When his cell phone rang, it made Dutch flinch and goose the accelerator. It was that familiar ringtone, the *Enter the Dragon* theme for Louie Mo. In this moment it sounded both ridiculous and macabre. Troy fished the cell from his jacket. "You all right?"

All he heard was strained breathing and random gun-shots, syncopated but deafening. Then the hoarse, broken, breathless English:

"You on bridge?"

"Yeah."

"Get the shot."

"*What?*"

"*You hear me,*" Louie spit. "When I hang up, ten sec-onds."

"Louie . . ."

The line went dead. Troy sat frozen for two seconds, knew he had only eight now. "Stop," he said.

Dutch braked at the far side of the bridge with a view straight out across to the top floors of the condemned apart-ments.

"Six seconds," he said.

He had the Arri propped in the open window, over-cranked and filming.

"He's gonna make the jump," Dutch said. "He led those fuckers inside, gonna blow them out."

• • •

Louie sprinted along what used to be the eighth-floor hall, but was now mostly crossbeams with occasional swatches of rotting plywood. He was headed for the open-sided east wall, which looked out onto a drab skyline and the skeletal neck of the rusted crane. Up here, he could smell chemicals and figured it was the chlorine Malone had talked about, an added ingredient to promote spectacular color in an explosion.

The Cantonese shouts behind him seemed more distant than he expected. He had outpaced these fuckers, they were sucking wind. Gunshots hit piping and cement, made Louie flinch, waiting for one errant shot to strike a C-4 canister before he can make his escape.

When he heard Tiger Eye's voice, cursing and grunting, he almost wanted to turn and face all of them. Fight it out. They were the guys who had ruined his life, really. But that's not what had been planned. He had promised the kid he was going to deliver his biggest stunt yet and here it beckoned, if he could just stay half a step ahead of the gunfire and time it right.

Four seconds . . . his heart is racing, blood pumping. His pupils dilate and everything out in front of him becomes otherworldly clear. Tunnel vision. He is feeling it now, the Creature in his bloodstream. It always surges harder when he's unwired, like now. Two seconds . . . but he's too far from the end of the beam and the timer tells him he's shit out of luck; that's when he comes alive, racing out ahead of the shock front, pulsing with that strange confidence that's carried him through his private war against gravity. As the building erupts—his eardrums rupture and ring—he feels himself launch from his body. No nets, no wires. This one's on him. And there's that question, somewhere just under the wild hum of the Creature and the ringing in his ears: Did I die this time?

• • •

Hektor jerked open the shot-up driver's-side door of the black van and struggled in, his wound throbbing. He knew he had to get out before the cops pulled in. When the old building exploded at the roof, he spun, almost fell. "*Madre de Christ*," he said in Spanglish as debris rained down. Cement chunks and twisted rebar slammed gravel nearby.

From the bridge, Troy watched through the wide-angle lens as the eighth floor ignited in blue flame and black dust. He wasn't sure what he was expecting, but he didn't anticipate the massive, sucking flicker, like a giant lightbulb blowing out. The bridge rumbled, but Troy aimed steady. He had the old crane in focus, waiting for Louie to clear the implosion, angry flames at his back, and land safely.

He never came out.

That's what Dutch kept saying now, bent toward the passenger-side window, watching. "Never came out. He never came out. Troy, he didn't make it."

Troy kept filming. Hoping. But when the top floor did just what Malone promised, pancaking onto the next floor down and creating a vertical domino collapse, he felt ill. Something told him to keep filming, that the moment he broke the shot there'd be no hope left. No Louie Mo magic. Only when he heard Dutch trying not to cry did he stop shooting and lower the big Arri.

"Stupid, brain-rattled motherfucker," she said. "Could have gotten out of town. Didn't have to do this."

Sirens were making short coyote yips in the distance, but Dutch kept the car idling on the bridge.

"He *had* to make it," Troy said. "He got out. I know it."

"Troy," she said, then she punched the gas angrily. They'd cross the bridge and take the side streets back to the 5. It was a shitty area in a dangerous 'hood. Dead ethnic gangbangers strewn outside a collapsed crack house wouldn't be a head scratcher for the LAPD. Shit, they'd probably be back at In-N-Out Burger an hour from now, bored by the whole affair.

Troy sat, turned around. He couldn't believe how neatly the building had come down, almost like someone had filmed its construction and then ran the film in reverse. He felt soiled having filmed it, knowing that people died inside. But he also felt the strong conviction of Louie Mo, knew what Louie had wanted. Maybe, Troy considered, leaving the world with one last crazy stunt was what he had planned all along.

• • •

Avi stood with a clutch of pedestrians at the corner of Ocean and Santa Monica, waiting for the little Crosswalk Man to appear. He felt his blood pressure rise as he thought about how he pitched the idea to Paramount and never heard back. Still, he had learned a long time ago how to harness anger into creativity and drive. He was already onto a new concept about bicycle cops called *Spokes*.

He also felt some compensation knowing that his Guatemalan investors had gone after Troy. They were going to kill the kid, toss him down a ditch in Malibu Canyon, that's what they'd said. *Slash* would be scrapped, but Avi would come out with a four-million-dollar profit and have these shady investors out of his life. Troy would take the fall, the little asshole deserved it. His dead body would actually be worth more than the finished movie.

Avi was already grooming a new kid, a fresh-faced guy named Dellasandro who had a film at Slamdance. He'd move him into the Las Flores beach house, cut a barter deal with him: a year's rent for a finished script and two-year option.

The light changed and Avi started to cross. He felt something hard in his ribs, felt warm breath at his ear.

He didn't have to look. He knew Hektor's voice, could scent the clove tobacco on his breath.

"Don't walk, motherfucker."

Avi smiled when he heard it, his own line, being called back at him. He deserved the riposte. He deserved it for trusting criminals; the bloodsuckers at the studios were no different from the drug dealers in Little San Salvador. He smiled at the irony, even as he was shoved into the backseat of the idling Buick. Even as the knife came out . . .

215

• • •

"I really loved that fucking guy, man."

Troy was on his seventh Corona, sitting around Dog House with the guys. With enough pizza to feed a rugby team, and empty Corona bottles lining the porch rail outside, the place had the bittersweet air of a family gathering after a funeral. Of course, there had been no funeral.

Dutch and Troy had reported the accidental death; city construction workers reported the charred and scattered remains in the rubble of the collapsed building. There was not enough for the medical examiner to make a positive ID, but the discovery was enough to produce a death certificate and an obituary that Troy, himself, had sent to the L.A. *Times*. It was an obit that Louie would have been proud of. In fact, the *Times* had to edit down Troy's eulogy, which featured an encyclopedic list of the Hong Kong movies Louie had worked on: *Black Cat, High Risk, The Bodyguard from Beijing, City on Flame, A Better Tomorrow II, Dragon Inn, Fist of Vengeance,* and *Farewell, Sweet Courtesan.* There were at least eighty more, but the list would have taken four columns. And who really cared?

Avi, meanwhile, had been spotted at the Coffee Bean with gauze taped over his left ear. Rumors said it had been cut off by certain disgruntled investors, and now he was named in a federal criminal complaint, charged with mail fraud. Turned out that he *could* get arrested after all. The fact that his victims were criminals themselves, however, gave his attorney some hope.

Troy took mercy on the producer, told him that although *Slash* was dead, he had something new in the can and would consider the one-hundred-and-eighty-grand budget—some of which he used on *The Cage*—an investment. Despite past tensions, Avi and Troy would remain partners. Sometimes the best work came out of such tensions, Avi said. "Any movie that's ever been a love fest to make has sucked ass."

"Better the cutthroat Armenian devil you know, than the

one you don't," Troy said, on beer number eight. "Besides, we've got to fight for Dog House."

"For Dog House," Malone battle-cried, hefting his Corona.

"For fucking Louie Mo," Troy said, clinking his bottle to Durbin's and then to T-Rich's empty.

They noticed her then. Standing barefoot in the open French doors, looking lost and windblown. Everyone grew quiet, like when spotting the widow at a wake. Malone finally said, "*Mahalo*," and Troy offered her a Corona, but she turned it down. She was holding a manila envelope like it was something foreign to her. She walked in, sank into Louie's favorite shabby-chic chair, and let a long sigh go.

"Went down to my post box," she said, tapping the envelope on her knee.

"What is it?"

"He had me drive him to some lawyer in North Hollywood a few times, times when he had a little cash. He didn't talk about it, but I just figured he was sending a few bucks back to Hong Kong. You know, to the Two-Headed Dragon."

She got quiet, looked toward the corner where the little apso was protectively gnawing on pizza crust. "Turns out, what he was actually doing was making quarterly payments. On a life insurance policy."

"You serious?"

"He took out a million dollars on his life. Named me as his, you know, his whatever."

For a moment, she looked like she was going to start

217

laughing more than cry. She did neither, just shook her head, shrugged, sank deeper in the chair.

"Dude, you were like a daughter to him," Troy said. "You took good care of him."

"And vice versa. Now I feel like I lost two dads, both crazy fuckers."

"A million dollars?"

She wasn't sure if Durbin said it, or T-Rich. She just nodded. There was a new Mustang that Louie knew she dreamed of, a sweetheart of a muscle ride. The old Chevy Impala was barely operable now, bullet-punched with hardly any glass left. She was going to buy the new car and start southeast, she said, back to Santa Fe.

It was her home and she was done running. Done hiding. Done with stunts, too. She was going back to find a certain cowboy, answer yes, and hope he still remembered the question. With a million bucks, they could buy a small ranch, breed quarter horses. Drive around in the pickup on Thursday mornings, cuddling with their coffees, check on newborn foals.

Troy told her that, no matter what, she always had a place at Dog House, and if she ever got a hankering to drive gags again, she was his girl.

"You honored him," Dutch said. "You gave him his pride back, you little film dweeb."

"He'd still be alive, though," Troy said, eyes on the floor. "Doing what?"

· · ·

DOG BEACH

He wanted to say good-bye to her in the morning, but he'd had too many beers, slept too hard. When he got up, she was gone. So was Louie's adopted lapdog. She had probably gone and bought that new Mustang, left her old beater in the lot. Gone east with a million dollars, the little white dog riding shotgun. Maybe Louie did know all along that he'd be going out with a bang. He had his papers in order. . . .

EPILOGUE

LE FESTIVAL DE CANNES—
EIGHT MONTHS LATER

Troy and Zoe sat drinking Bellinis at Le 72 on the seaside Croisette Promenade, just across from the Martinez Hotel. A warm Mediterranean breeze played in Zoe's bangs. She was dressed for the post-screening party in a little black number and heels. Troy wore a rumpled white linen jacket over a black tee, blue jeans, and two-toned leather flats without socks. His cheeks were sunburned to a gloss, hers were mocha tan.

It had been nine days of sun, sex, and celebrities—quite a few, like George Clooney, telling Troy how much they enjoyed *The Cage*. Clooney singled out Zoe's one scene, told her she reminded him of a young Sonia Braga. He then asked her if she did hot yoga because she looked like the type who did hot yoga. Troy watched her eyes as Clooney walked off. He knew that if George had said, "Young lady, let's go across to the Martinez and fuck like fruit bats until the closing ceremonies," she would have gathered her clutch purse and abandoned Troy Raskin at Le 72. Or maybe not.

Troy didn't care.

Nor did he care that Clooney had used the word "enjoyed," a euphemism that Troy had learned about from Avi. "If someone says, 'I enjoyed it,' what they really mean is 'It blows, but I'm being polite, even though you know what I really think.'"

He laughed when he said it, and Zoe liked that, this new sense of humor. The old Troy would have said something vindictive. Or had an asthma attack. Tonight, at Le Festival de Cannes, he was simply feeling invincible.

Harvey Weinstein liked the movie—didn't enjoy it, really *liked* it—and was already talking to the young ICM agent Troy had signed with, even as CAA agents were staking him out three tables away. Relativity Media wanted to buy in and so did Lionsgate, his agent texted. *We're going to make a lot of money together*, said the text.

"If only he was here to see this," Troy said, swirling his drink around slowly in the tall, fluted glass.

"Louie?"

Troy nodded, watching paparazzi flashing cameras at someone leaving the Martinez. At the screening two nights before, in the Théâtre Lumière, a brief tribute to the stuntman Louie Mo had received a mix of enthusiastic applause and laughter. An outtake from *The Cage*, in which Louie hits a Muay Thai boxer in the chops, apologizes, then winks into the camera, nearly brought down the house. However, the big climax of the movie itself, when Cho is trapped in an old building and killed in an explosion . . .

DOG BEACH

The crowd had grown uncomfortably still, watching the flames rooster-tail from the roof as the structure imploded and pancaked downward. Normally, a filmmaker would cut this shot, but Troy's opening speech explained why it would remain. The audience reaction to the scene was more akin to watching high art than to watching the money scene of a popcorn flick. To know that a man died in the explosion, trying to achieve the greatest stunt of a forgotten career, it got to people. Even those who merely "enjoyed it" did not escape unmoved by the third-act climax.

The final shot was just the blank desert. Troy shot it in Antelope Valley, at the magic hour, right where he had planned to film Louie walking away; a gunfighter who'd outlived his era.

Instead, Troy filmed a sidewinder of a breeze on the dirty sand, played Louie's prerecorded voiceover about breaking out of "the cages we build for ourselves."

Watching it that night in the Lumière, three seats over from a sleeping Lars von Trier, Troy wished so badly that Louie really had walked away, dazed and damaged, perhaps, but no worse for wear. Louie had once described himself as a cat who had lived nine lives; Troy wished Louie would have defied the rule and gone for one more. He fantasized, during the end credits and the applause, that Louie was sitting in a Santa Clarita diner somewhere, telling jokes to a plump waitress and trying to buy painkillers from truck drivers.

"I'm wicked proud of you," Zoe said, snapping Troy from his haze. He could see the Bellini shining in her black eyes.

She was feeling it. Her lips were doing something remarkable with a peach slice.

"Wanna go back to the room?" she said.

"What time is the Soderbergh screening?"

"Who gives a fuck?"

"That's what I say."

She picked up her clutch and they'd started to leave when Troy's cell phone rang. It was sitting on the table, a few inches from his drained Bellini. The ringtone stopped him dead.

Troy felt himself caught in a freeze-frame, saw Zoe half-turning with her little purse, a warm breeze in her bangs. The sound of ferryboats, young women laughing in German, the scent of French loaves. The cell kept ringing. *Enter the Dragon*: old-school jazz and a jungle scream . . .

In memory of Ju Kun,
legendary stuntman and friend